Conflicts

G. Burns Hamilton

AOS Publishing, 2024
Copyright © 2024

G. Burns Hamilton

ISBN: 978-1-990496-72-1

Cover Design: Chanelle Poupart

Visit AOS Publishing's website:
www.aospublishing.com

“Nothing is more noble, nothing more venerable,
than loyalty”

-- Cicero

Table of Contents

Glossary

APC – Armoured Personnel Carrier.

BMP – A Russian type of APC.

Boma – An enclosure, especially for animals.

CWO – Chief Warrant Officer.

EO – Executive Outcomes. A private military company that was founded in 1989 and ceased to operate in 1998.

FBO – Fixed Base Operator. An organization operating an airport to provide services such as refuelling. Most frequently used by corporate jets and other small aircraft.

FIB – Fuse instantaneous burning. A cable type fuse with an ignition rate of several thousand feet per second.

Five Eyes – An intelligence alliance composed of Australia, Canada, New Zealand, the United Kingdom, and the United States.

FN P90 – A compact 5.7×28mm submachine gun.

JTF2 – Joint Task Force Two. The Canadian special forces unit.

Laager – A temporary fortification made of trucks or armoured vehicles arranged into a rectangle, circle, or other shape to produce an improvised military camp.

LAW – Light Anti-tank Weapon.

Linear Shaped Charge – A shaped charge is an explosive charge shaped to focus the effect of the explosive's energy. A linear shaped charge focuses the energy along a line.

P320 – A Sig Sauer handgun.

PPCLI – Princess Patricia Canadian Light Infantry.

RPG – Rocket Propelled Grenade.

RUF – The Revolutionary United Front (RUF) was a rebel group that fought a failed eleven-year war in Sierra Leone, beginning in 1991 and ending in 2002.

RV – Military short form for rendezvous. Used to define a location to assemble or meet, as in RV point, or time as in RV at 18:00.

SAW – Squad Automatic Weapon – a light machine gun.

SUPU – Supplementary Power Unit.

SWAPO – South-West Africa People's Organisation. The independence movement in Namibia.

UNITA – União Nacional para a Independência Total de Angola. A communist party led by Jona Savimbi that fought a civil war in Angola from 1975 until 2002.

UNPROFOR – The UN peacekeeping force operating in the Balkans 1992-1995.

UNTAG – The UN Transition Assistance Group. UNTAG was established by the UN to ensure the orderly independence of Namibia in 1989-1990.

Chapter 1.
James - January

Fuck, what is wrong with me? I can barely move. Was I in an accident? Why is my face wet?

I was lying flat face-down on the ground, on cement or stone. Slowly, I tried to lift my head, to see where I was, but there was hardly any light in the room. Giving up, I let my head back down to rest. After waiting for my breath to slow, I agonizingly used my right arm to push me over onto my back, then passed out for a while.

As I opened my eyes the second time, I could see that I was in a small, stone room with light coming in from a tiny, barred window, high on one wall. *Fuck*, everything rushed back – I was in the old slave prison on Wailing Island. Oh, man, this is bad. This place is a hellhole.

I struggled to sit up and take in the room; stone with a nasty, mossy slime on the walls. A hole in the stone floor in the corner, stained black all around, was unmistakably the toilet.

It was all coming back now. One, two, or three days ago, I was called to the office of the President of Doadja, Theodoro Obissey. We had been business partners since shortly after I moved my base of operations here seven years ago. While I don't spend much time here, it has been a perfect spot to build my business, with protection provided by the national government. I have a nice house, with a large staff, and I am not worried about safety, but this horrible little country is hot, humid, and unhealthy. It is a dictatorship that is poor as a rat because the President loots the country, treating the national treasury as his own personal piggy bank.

The upside is that I have a free hand here to do whatever business I want – arms trading or anything else that comes along. The arms trading is made easy by my partnership with the

President – Doadja issues end-user certificates to provide cover for the weapons I move to other countries. This freedom comes at a price.

When I arrived at the Palace a few days ago, his Chief of Staff, Austin Mbaye, met me.

"Any idea what he wants?" I asked.

"He will tell you himself, come with me."

It didn't take a second after entering the big guy's office to sense that something was wrong, he was in a rage.

"James, what don't you understand about Doadja? I told you how things work here. Now you have really pissed me off," President Obissey raged.

"What's the issue, what can I do to make it right, Mr. President?"

"You can be an example to others," he said.

Suddenly, four of the Presidential Guard thugs came into the room. One clipped me on the head with a night-stick, and another whacked my knees with his. *And here I am, beaten, locked up, and not even sure what day it is. They clearly worked me over well before dumping me here.*

The two main issues right now are – what was it that pissed him off, and how do I get out of here?

In terms of annoying el Presidente, the possibilities of what he may be thinking include: I am under-reporting the arms sales net income; I possibly dated a woman that he had his eye on; someone like the EU has been putting pressure on to stop the arms business; I have been talking to his potential political opponents; he is entitled to some revenue from my other business here, or maybe he thinks I am getting too rich and too powerful in his country.

So, quite a few possibilities; but in this cell, it is going to be hard to find out more. I can only hope that Sabi starts to notice my absence, because of my lack of communication, and starts asking questions. If he can find out what the problem is, he may be able to solve it. Bribery is routine here, although bribing Mr. Big will clearly be a challenge involving millions of dollars. The bastard is already a multi-billionaire. The bribe itself will mean nothing to his wealth but will simply have to be large enough to obviously hurt me.

What about bribing others, like Austin? Hmm, he wouldn't take any action that could annoy the president in any case. Bribing army General Yalumba is a remote possibility – he would have to be ready to take on the risk of overthrowing Obissey. That would be extremely dangerous for both of us, and he has never shown any courage. Bribing the Colonel that runs the prison, or the General that heads the Presidential Guard, would involve a considerable risk of death for everyone implicated. The Guard general is also Obissey's cousin.

On the other hand, staying here is not an option. This prison on Wailing Island was built by the French using slave labour back in the 1700s. It was really meant as an assembly and transshipment point for slaves destined for the Caribbean or South America. By combining a large army barracks on the landside of the island with this slave prison on the open ocean side, it was meant to be secure. Health and survival, however, were never a consideration. The damp and moldy cells, along with rats and mosquitoes, have always meant an alarming death rate here, even now.

Everything I have heard about this dungeon since I set up in Doadja has been bad news.

Not that anybody cares. Today, there is a mix in here of actual criminals and anybody else that even looks like they could be a problem for Obissey. Just having an education can be enough to get you in here. I can't think of anyone that has been released. There may have been a few lucky ones. If you have been in here, you want to keep an extremely low profile in case you ever get out. Leaving the country would be the best choice.

Has anyone escaped? Not that I know of. On the ocean side, it is a sheer drop into high surf against the stone wall. Access on the land side is through the army battalion base, then across the bridge to the mainland. The gap to the mainland isn't that wide – about three hundred metres, but before anyone could try to swim the gap, they would have to get through the army base. It might be possible, but with a low chance of success.

Well, this altogether sucks. There's nothing to do but wait for Sabi to do something.

I seriously wish I had never ended up in Doadja, but the downside with the arms trade is that there aren't many countries where it is possible to set up operations. If you are from Russia, or some of the other old Eastern Bloc countries, you can set up base there, but if you are from one of the Western democracies, they don't want you operating from their countries. The Americans are happy to deal with you when they need arms delivered to a friend and don't want a visible link to the CIA, but they wouldn't consider allowing you to operate from the US. They preferred dealing with me over some of the established operators, because they knew I wasn't selling to terrorist groups. My trade was almost entirely within Africa, and more recently, with groups in Myanmar.

When I first started and was just a sub-agent, I didn't have a base. I was primarily getting arms for mercenary groups that I was working with, and I would go to the usual old Russian players to get weapons and ammunition. As my business grew, I needed a place to set up my base. I started in Nairobi. Great climate, mostly rule of law, some okay housing, with good bars and restaurants. That worked for a while, then the rule of law thing started to become a problem. The Brits and the French started to notice my business and put pressure on the Kenyan government to shut me down, so it was time to get out of town.

The draw for me in Doadja was the complete lack of rule of law. The country has no friends, and no geopolitical interest from the big dog states as long as the oil keeps flowing. The President of Doadja simply doesn't care what any other country thinks of him. Although the major countries comment from time to time about the poor state of human rights in Doadja, they don't care enough to limit the travel of the ruling family. They have major estates in multiple European countries that are simply ignored. So, Doadja sounded like a great base for the arms trade.

When I first got here, I operated low key, but following the offer from Obissey that I couldn't refuse, it didn't take me long to see that this presented a bigger opportunity. With Obissey, I could grow my business, JaMAC, even faster. End-user certificates issued by Obissey would create some impression of legitimacy for my acquisition and movement of weapons. He was greedier than I even imagined, but otherwise it was okay. The day we met, I had no trouble recognizing him, because his picture is everywhere in Doadja – every office, every business, even in homes. The pictures always have him in some sort of uniform or ceremonial dress, but even in a suit jacket and open collar shirt he was easily recognizable. Not many people in Doadja have the pudgy appearance of someone with an oversupply of food and wine. His many gold rings and oversized Jaeger-LeCoultre watch completed the picture of a "big man."

Austin, his Chief of Staff, stayed in the room and took notes.

"Mr. President, I am James MacKenzie. I have been a resident here for some weeks and I intend to grow a business here."

"I know who you are, James, and I know what you have been up to. That is why I sent for you. You know that your business could cause problems for Doadja?"

"Of course, sir. I shouldn't cause you problems without also bringing you some benefit."

"What are you proposing?" he asked.

"I expect that you know my kind of business can be exceptionally profitable, sir. I am proposing that I would pay you a commission, or agent fee of twenty percent of profits. In return, you would be flexible in issuing end-user certificates to, you know, build up the Doadjan forces.”

“Hmm, here is what will happen, James. I will become a fifty percent shareholder of your business, this JaMAC. We will audit the accounts. Austin will draw up the agreement.”

“Fifty percent seems steep, sir. What do I get by giving up this fifty percent, why don’t I just move to another country?”

“Because I will let you operate from Doadja without a problem, and because I will have end-user certificates provided to you that will enable you to grow OUR business.

“James, do not play with me. I am the law here. If you don’t like the deal, go back to Nairobi. You have a unique opportunity here. We will look the other way while you stockpile here and deal with whoever you want, except of course me, exclusively with respect to Doadja.”

“Sir, the deal seems fine to me. I look forward to getting Austin’s document and will make appropriate changes to the shareholding.”

“Excellent, James, I look forward to seeing the cash flow from your business. Talk to Austin whenever you need certificates from us.”

So, that’s what has happened for the past seven years, until this week’s meeting. It worked well, until it didn’t, and that’s how I ended up here.

The day was slipping away, and the room was getting darker. It was never especially light in any case, with the single small window high on the wall, but I could tell it was heading toward evening. There was a rattling metallic noise and a slot opened at the base of the door. A tin bowl with a spoon in it was slid into the room.

What was in the bowl was gross – a film of grease on top of a watery broth with some grains of rice and a bit of unknown greenery.

"Hey, is this it - no bread, nothing more?" I shouted.

There was the sound of a rifle butt banging on my door.

"Hey, you in there, you shut right up. You make any noise, we come in there and we beat you good. You just sit there and think about your death."

I didn't think I could even bring myself to eat that cold mess in the bowl, but hunger just pushes you forward. I don't even know what the grease was from, there was no meat that I could detect. It was like someone had dumped some palm oil into the water.

I really needed Sabi to get me out of here. There was no one else in Doadja that would be interested in helping me. There are some old friends in Canada who would try to help but they won't even know what has happened to me. It all comes down to Sabi.

I know Sabi must be trying to get me out, but it better be soon. He is incredibly loyal and my best friend since I left the army. We have been through a lot of challenging times together, but always managed to pull through.

Sabi and I go back to '95 when I finished a tour with the UN in Namibia. I had discovered that I loved Africa and that the Canadian military bored me. Underequipped and mostly doing UN stuff, it was like standing in the middle of a boxing ring with your hands tied behind your back. It wasn't what I wanted. I started looking for mercenary opportunities in Africa. It took a couple of months of searching. The types of jobs I was looking for are not posted on LinkedIn, or as ads in the paper. Eventually I got connected to Executive Outcomes in the UK and they sent me to Angola. That's where I met Sabi.

We were together in Angola only briefly. The mercenary crowd in that country was originally there to train the government troops, but it became more effective to simply lead the fighting against UNITA, the communist rebel party led by Jonas Savimbi. The government troops weren't really an army, more like an untrained gang.

When I first showed up, there was some clear pushback from the mercenaries already on the ground, many of whom had experience in-country with the South Africans. "Who was this white dude coming in as an officer, what did he know? I got approval from higher-ups to pull a company of Angolan soldiers out of the line so that I could spend two weeks training them. Sabi came with me as my CWO. He was smart, experienced, and had a great can-do attitude. I started the two weeks by telling the group that my job was not only to make them effective, but to keep them alive while being effective (they liked that). Sabi and I worked them hard on range work – the way they were spraying bullets all over the place when I arrived, it was almost impossible to keep them supplied. We worked on tactics, and movement as well. At the end of that training we took them up-country around Huambo where, augmented with some additional mercenaries, we were brutally effective at shutting Savimbi's boys down.

As we wound down operations in Angola, Sierra Leone and Liberia came to life. That's the thing about Africa, there is always a firefight going on somewhere. There is always someone trying to overthrow a government, or someone else is trying to seize a diamond field or a coltan mine.

Angola was crazy and definitely dangerous, but nothing compared to Sierra Leone. I am sometimes surprised that we both survived that. It was the insane randomness of the violence that made it so fucking dangerous. Buffoons wearing amulets that they believed made them bulletproof could suddenly come out of the woods and just start killing everyone in sight. The amount of AK fire and RPG fire in some of the firefights was astounding. It was *Mad Max* in the forest.

The RUF seemed to have an almost unlimited ammo supply, and for a while nobody in EO knew what the RUF's logistics were. Because they were moving everything by foot, their major supply point couldn't be far – a day or two's walk at most.

I don't know the source, but the location was uncovered, and I was assigned to take Sabi and three others to get in and blow up this stockpile. The idea was simple. Although this logistics centre would be guarded and have lots of movement, they would not expect a deep penetration several days' walk behind their lines.

The trek into the forest was straight forward. It was a small group of pros (we had been together since Angola, three of the guys had served with the SA special forces), so we moved silently and were constantly wary of what was going on around us. Although we did use bush paths, the RUF were so undisciplined that we had lots of warning when a group was coming on the path, so we would simply drift off into the bush without a word and take up hiding positions while the chattering clowns walked past.

We only had a few stops like this because of potential interaction. We grabbed maybe five hours' sleep and some cold food during the first night. We approached the laager after two days as predicted. We could hear it from a long way away. Lots of voices, sounds of vehicles, even occasional gunfire. It was late afternoon. I signaled to the guys to settle in while I made my way forward to take a look around.

It had been a small village. There were a handful of mud houses with thatched roofs. Converting it to their centre, RUF had created a kind of boma, with a thornbush wall perimeter. There was a lot of movement. Really hard to tell, but it looked like fifty to seventy RUF hanging out, off-loading trucks, etc. From time-to-time, small groups would come into the compound, and be greeted with chat. That explained the gunfire we had heard. A group would show up and someone would celebrate the arrival of old buds with a burst of AK fire into the air.

The stockpiles were impressive. In addition to cases after cases of small arms cartridges, there were boxes of mortars, RPGs, grenades, even C4. I have no idea where these goofs were getting the money for this. Diamonds probably. In any case, that wasn't our problem today. We were here to disrupt their ops for a week or more by blowing this stuff.

I made my way back to the troops, pulled them together, and whispered a plan as dark fell.

"Guys, there are maybe fifty RUF in there. As usual, they are smoking dope and getting drunk, so they will be crap at dawn."

I paused and, using a stick, drew a rough sketch of the layout on the ground.

"The perimeter should be easy to breach with RPG fire. It may even be possible to simply push aside the temporary closures at the gates, especially if their guards are asleep or not even there. There are two openings. One closest to us, is the route that the RUF uses between here and the front. The other, on the opposite side, is the bush road entrance where trucks are coming in bringing supplies."

"We will move in the dark up close to the boma. Sabi, you take Leon, and Bami, and breach on this side. Hit at soldier's light while the RUF are going to have trouble figuring out who is who!"

I pointed to the map.

"As soon as you are in, focus on your left, on the east side of the compound. There is a large stockpile of crated RPGs there. Hit that with everything until it blows. If we light that up, it's going to take out a large part of the supplies and RUF. Keep up heavy fire, I want you to draw as much of the RUF as you can. Olivier and I will come through the road gap on the other side, we will also work left and our focus will be the stocks of C4 and grenades. The plan is to get enough destruction from the demolition of the RPG, C4, and grenade stocks to light up the small arms crates as well. We will wait until you have hit the RPG stocks to attack from the other side. Keep your fire left of twelve o'clock and we will be doing the same. We don't want any friendly fire incidents. The plan is for you to draw most of the fire."

Sabi laughed.

"I knew that would be the plan."

The others chuckled as well.

"Only keep up the fire until you see we have set off the stocks that I am targeting on the west side, then withdraw. Move fast. Olivier and I will need to take a circuitous route around the boma, so we will be behind you by an hour or more. Let's meet up just north of that abandoned village we passed yesterday around fifteen hundred. We will stick to the path as we approach that area – keep an eye out and hail us."

"I expect both groups may have tails. This is really going to shake RUF. I am hoping that they are so disrupted that it takes them a while to get organized. Watch your backs and move as quickly as you safely can."

"Any questions?"

"James, any chance we won't be able to get these stockpiles blowing up?" asked Bami.

"The RPG stocks will be easy, if you hit them with a few RPGs, they are going to go up. The C4 and grenades are more challenging. If we can't get them going with RPG fire, I am going to go in and set a charge in the C4 stocks. Olivier will provide cover fire.

"Okay, let's settle in, I will roust everyone around 0430."

In the dark early morning, I silently shook each of the soldiers. Olivier and I headed out first. Moving in the dark in the bush while keeping quiet was slow going, but we were set up before dawn near the road entrance. I could see that the RUF had dragged two temporary wood and bush gates across the road. They weren't even completely closed. There looked to be enough space to squeeze through without even moving them. No sign of a patrol - either sleeping off a drunk nearby or not even posted.

In that half-light we call soldier's light, Sabi's group opened up. There was complete chaos, as they fired everything they had at the RPG stocks. There was almost no return fire. The RUF seemed dumbfounded. Olivier and I just got up and walked through the opening in the gate. The RUFfians were scrambling up and were all looking north at the fire coming from Sabi's group. Olivier took the initiative – he is a native South African. He started to yell at the RUF nearest us,

"Get up, go, go, go we are under attack. Get in there."

He was waving them forward. Confused and hung over, they all started firing toward the north side of the compound and running in that direction. Then the RPG stocks ignited. A big part of the compound just vanished.

I walked over to the piles of C4 crates, used my bayonet to pry open a case, took out the sticks, and pitched it. Reaching into my own pack, I pulled out a prepped charge, with a detonator and roll of det cord attached, and stuffed it into the case, then trotted back through the gate unreeling the det cord.

Olivier had kept up his encouragement and no one was paying any attention to me. When he saw that I was clear of the gate, he ran back to join me; we dropped into one of the ruts of the road, put our heads down, and I set off the charge. The initial blast of C4 was followed by all kinds of secondary explosions as crates of grenades went off. Not a whole lot was left of the compound. Olivier and I got up to leave when a truck came up behind us, heading to the compound. RUF started bailing out and firing on us.

"Change of plan, Olivier, through the compound!"

We ran back into the compound which was really a burning hell at that point. We tried to use the confusion to work our way through the RUF that were prone, firing on Sabi's group, but this was clearly going to unravel, and we couldn't slow down or the truck guys were going to get us, so we took cover and simply started shooting RUF. I covered the truck guys and Sabi faced the other way. Not good, taking fire from all directions. Luckily, the RUF were just not that good. But we were pinned into the spot.

That's when Sabi came to our rescue. Seeing what had happened, which was amazing, because the whole laager was a sea of flame and smoke, Sabi just led his guys forward. I don't know how many RUF were killed in the blasts, but between Sabi's group, Olivier, and me, we eliminated the rest of them. Even with the RUF all down, the compound was a nightmare with a barrage of small arms cartridges cooking off from the heat of the fires.

Sabi came up to us smiling;

"Good to see you, boss. I was just ready to pull out and start for home when I saw your whitey face in the middle of the damn compound. Oh, no, I said to myself, I have to save his hopeless ass once again."

In that rush of adrenaline, the whole group started laughing. Even Bami, who had taken a hit on his shoulder and was busy bandaging it up.

"Well done, guys, let's head for home. We have a two-day hike ahead of us, and not everyone on the trail will be friendly.

Anyway, the Western organized mercenary groups were pushed out of Angola and Sierra Leone by the UN. They were replaced on the ground by UN troops that were completely useless in maintaining the peace. Sabi and I moved on to the Congo, working in mine security and protection. Contrary to what one might think, mine protection in the Congo is not a bunch of lightly-armed security guards hanging around a gate house, it's an actual continuation of mercenary work. Heavily armed, we didn't just protect the mine site, we moved into the countryside to eliminate the groups that were attacking the mine. It was chaos. Almost every neighbouring country was backing some group or another. There were completely out of control murderers, often destroying villages just for the pure hell of it. It was very hard to make any sense of what was driving things, other than money and power.

It was in the Congo that Sabi and I started moving into the weapons trade. We started by working to get weapons for our own units, then we began to supply other friendlies. Sabi worked the friendly end and I worked the sources in Russia, Bulgaria, and Georgia. If there was money available, we found that we could get anything – assault rifles, machine guns, mortars, RPGs, APCs, even armour. It was all just a matter of dollars and logistics – how to get the weapons to where you wanted them to go.

Anyway, that's why I have so much faith in Sabi. He is my friend of more than twenty-five years, my brother in arms, and a significant shareholder in JaMAC. If anyone can get me out of here, it will be Sabi.

Chapter 2.
Sabi - January

Where is James? He was called to see the President on Tuesday and I didn't see him after that. Maybe he went directly to the airport and took his plane to do something for the President. He could have headed off somewhere with the President. This has happened before. He doesn't make a point of keeping me informed of his comings and goings. I should call the airport.

"Louis, it's Sabi. Is James' pilot there?"

"Sure, one minute"

"Robert here."

"Bob, it's Sabi, have you seen James, or taken him anywhere?"

"Not since the week before last. I haven't heard from him since we got back from France."

"Okay, thanks. Let me know if he gets in touch."

So, that means he is in-country. He almost never heads off by land to any of the nearby countries. He has disappeared for two or three days before. When that happens, he is typically shacked up with a local woman that he met in a bar here.

I started calling hotels, beginning with the Continental, really the only hotel in town that even pretends to serve Western guests. We have no tourism in Doadja, and the only business visitors are oil guys. They most often stay at one of their company guest houses in a fenced compound.

No luck at the Continental. They knew James and would have told me if he was there. I tried a few other hotels, including some in the smaller towns outside the capital. Again, no luck.

James doesn't seem to be shacked up somewhere. Typically, when he does that, it is three days max. The other possibility is that for some reason he is still at the Palace.

I called Austin at the Palace.

"Good morning, it's Sabi Issa at JaMAC, can I talk to the Chief of Staff please?"

'One moment."

"Mr. Issa, the Chief of Staff is unavailable at this time."

"Okay, thank you. Please ask him to call me back. You know my number. I am trying to locate James Mackenzie. I haven't been able to reach him since he met with the President on Tuesday."

"Fine, goodbye."

I suppose James could have had an accident. It seems unlikely, it wasn't that far to the Palace from the JaMAC offices and the traffic is slow, but I checked.

"Nambi General Hospital, how can I assist you?"

"Do you have a patient called James Mackenzie? White, about sixty years old. He would have been admitted on Tuesday."

"One moment."

"We have no James Mackenzie admitted – in fact, no white patients at all, currently."

"Thanks very much."

Next step...

"Doadja Police, may I help you?"

"I am trying to locate James Mackenzie. You probably know who I mean – white guy, well-dressed, and middle-aged. He has been missing since Tuesday."

"That's only four days, sir."

"I know, but I am his number two and he typically would let me know where he is going. Any possibility that you are holding him?"

"No whites in holding."

"Can you put out a notice that he is missing?"

"No, not after only four days. Call us back next week if there is still no sign of him."

Crap, no leads at all. The only time he disappeared for a few days without letting me know in advance was two years ago when he met that major player from Lebanon at the airport and they left on the other guy's plane to go to Libya. He turned up on the fourth day when he was dropped back here.

One more step that I haven't tried. I went to James' computer and looked at his schedule. Nothing showing.

Strange that I couldn't connect with Austin. I considered who else at the Palace might know what happened after the meeting. I thought of the Presidential Guard, but those pricks were all from Obissey's tribe, arrogant, and most likely to tell me to piss off.

Time to try Austin again, but in person. I took a taxi over to the Palace. At the gatehouse, I asked the guard to call the Chief of Staff and tell him that Sabi Issa was here, asking for a brief meeting. I sat waiting with others, sitting on one of the many chairs along the wall. Eventually, the phone rang, and after a brief conversation, the guard waved me over.

"Mr. Austin is not available."

"That's it – no more information about come back later, or anything."

"Mr. Austin is not available, that's all I know."

This is starting to look bleak. In the past, Austin, while not a friend, was at least cognizant of the partnership between James and the President, and would call me back the same day and see me the next day. This points to a problem between James and Obissey.

Just outside the palace gates, there is a permanent outdoor market of about forty stalls, with fish, vegetables, fruit, some leather goods, a little meat.

Not a tourist place, because there are no tourists, but a simple market for the locals. Tourists wouldn't be impressed in any case, with the fresh but unrefrigerated meat and fish swarming with flies. The blowing dust coating all the stands didn't make anything look more appetizing, either.

But these same stall operators are here every day and see whatever comes and goes from the palace, so I started up one side, asking if they had seen James.

"Brother, I am missing my white partner. Did you happen to see any palace comings and goings of a white guy this week?"

"No, man, I don't pay any attention to palace coming and going. Better just to mind myself. Nothing good comes from being interested in the palace."

I started to work my way up the row and was at the fourth stall, when I received a sharp poke in the back.

"What you up to?"

I turned, and there was a Presidential Guard member. The poke in my back was apparently from his assault rifle, since it was now pointed at my belly.

"Just trying to locate a friend."

"Well, you be better off moving away from here now."

"Okay, no worries, I'm leaving." *My approach is that the person with the rifle is always right.*

I waited until Sunday. Still nothing. Time to start working informal networks. Who had the best in-country networks – somebody that has strong tribal links? I called Michel.

"Michel, it's Sabi Issa."

"Hello, Sabi, long time, how's it going? What brings you to call?"

"Michel, I am trying to find my boss, James. You know James."

"Sure, everybody knows James. There aren't many white guys that stay in Doadja for more than a week or two – at least, white guys that aren't Lebanese."

"He isn't perfect at keeping me informed, but he has been missing for almost a week. He was called to see the President last Tuesday, and then radio silence ever since."

"Being called to see the President isn't necessarily a good thing."

"Yes, I know, but I called Austin at the Palace and he hasn't returned my call."

"Not a good thing, either. Did you try the police, all that?"

"Of course – hospital, police. I didn't try the Presidential Guard because I am not part of that Obissey network."

"Yes, that would have been pointless. How can I help?"

"You have a large network in the tribe. Can you circulate the word to all the families and see if anyone knows where he is? I checked the airport, and it doesn't look like he left the country. He is here somewhere."

"Sure, but you owe me one. You never call except when you need something. You need to take me out for some beers and some music sometime soon."

"I can do that, but let's find James first. Do you need a picture or something, or more info?"

"Nah, people know who James is. But this will take a few days to get the network working."

"Okay, Thanks, Michel, talk to you."

Nothing from anyone until the following Thursday.

"Sabi, it's Michel. Your guy is on Wailing Island."

"Oh, man, that is seriously bad. How do you know?"

"It took a while, but through my nephew's wife we turned up a prison guard that saw him being dragged in."

"Dragged?"

"Yes, dropped off by the Presidential Guard assholes, all beaten up."

"Shit, he must have had some kind of issue with Obissey."

"Only possible explanation."

"Well, not good news, but thanks for tracking this down. At least I know where he is."

"Watch your own back, Sabi, if you are going to ask around. If the big guy is angry at James, he might not be too happy to see you, either. Give me a call for our beers together. Bye."

Obissey isn't irrational, but anything that even remotely might challenge his power or wealth is dangerous. It is just a fact of life here. This would be one empty country if people could afford to migrate. On the other hand, it is that lack of laws that made it a cool place for James and me to operate.

I was really on my own to try and get James out. In Doadja, I was really his only friend. None of the stream of casual girlfriends he has had here would give a rat's ass about him. He has no legal representation here, and that would be pointless in any case. Nothing in the company material indicated that he had a criminal lawyer in Canada that might help.

What about friends in Canada? I knew he didn't see much of them, but I had heard him late afternoons from time to time on Zoom, Facebook, WhatsApp, Lime, or whatever... talking to old friends.

Going into James' office, I saw his laptop on the desk. James wasn't aware that I knew his password, but fortunately, with a view to looking out for number one, I do have it - RMC12076!

I pulled up Outlook and went through his contacts. Most of them were our clients - the bad-news crowd of arms dealers and criminals. I needed to whittle it down. I put Canada in the search box, and about twelve names popped up. Some were routine contacts for whenever he went back there, which he did once and a while - drugstore, doctor, property manager (he kept a condo in Toronto). But there were a couple of others that looked promising: Nadeem Nawaz, showing as Director General, Africa with Canadian Government [GAC]; and Matthew Hawney, Canadian Communications Security Establishment.

Both had nicknames in their Outlook address entries (Nad, Mato), suggesting that these were personal friends, not business contacts.

I drafted an email and sent it off to those two:

I am Sabi Issa. I work with James Mackenzie and am using his email in his absence to draw attention to his situation.

I believe that you are a friend of James. He was arbitrarily imprisoned here in Doadja on the twelfth of January. You may be aware that there is no legal system here and that mechanisms that you might normally use in Canada, involving a legal approach to determine the cause, arranging bail, preparing for a trial, etc., are not an option here.

As you know, James is not married, and because of his extensive travel, he does not have a network of friends here in Doadja. He would typically turn to me for help, and I have done what I can, but without any success. The only information I have is that this surprise arrest is the direct result of a possible disagreement with the President of Doadja, Theodoro Obissey.

That is why I am seeking your advice and help. I notice that you are, or have been, in senior positions with the Canadian government and may be able to apply some external pressures, or even make inquiries that could help in getting James released.

Please be aware that being imprisoned here is a life-threatening situation, so the longer James is there, the less likely he will survive. The prison here is a two-hundred-year-old disease-ridden slave prison, and the fatality rate is extremely high. To my knowledge, almost no one is ever released.

Anything you can do to help would be appreciated. I have worked under James in one form or another since 1995 and am his best friend here in Doadja.

Chapter 3.
Nadeem - January

Like most working people, I check my emails frequently. The first thing that I did that morning was open my inbox, and I could see an email titled "Friend Needs Help." Checking the sender address, I saw that it was from James Mackenzie. Strange, I hadn't heard from James for quite a while. Occasionally, when he was back in Toronto briefly, he would give me a call. Sometimes it worked out that we could get together for dinner and a catch-up. We had a bit of a ritual. We would meet at Opus, a high-end traditional restaurant near his hotel and James would order wines that I could never afford. With the great service and amazing wines, we would simply enjoy the dinner and talk late into the evening.

Ever since he became Africa-based, visits have been few and far between.

The email indicated that James was in prison and had been for the past few weeks or more, in one of the worst countries in Africa. Probably, the worst in the world. A local employee or partner named Sabi Issa (a local Doadja name), is seeking help in trying to free James.

James' situation rang a particular bell with me because I have lived in Africa and am very familiar with life there. Doadja, I already knew, was one of the worst African dictatorships. But why would James be imprisoned there? The only thing I could think of was something to do with his arms trading business.

I see that Mato, Matt Hawney, was also copied on the email. It's obvious that Issa had grabbed the names from James' Outlook list, because the common link is our time together at the Royal Military College, and subsequently in the Canadian Forces.

James, Mato, and I were close in those years. The college had a way of bringing people together, even people of disparate backgrounds. The stresses, shared challenges of life at the college, and the combat training during the summers, created a "band of brothers" feeling. It's hard to explain, but after those four intense years together at RMC (1979 to 1983), and then service time, you get to know some of your classmates better than anyone else you will ever meet. You know absolutely that they would risk their life for you. In some cases, this has even been proven.

When I say that the college brought people together, I don't mean an extensive network of the whole class. Typically, those that started within the same squadron, and that were in the same service can develop close bonds. Even though the three of us had really divergent backgrounds, and went on to live quite different lives, it didn't prevent those bonds from forming and lasting.

James was the most different from the rest of us, in terms of his youth. He grew up as an army brat, moving frequently, with no real hometown. From what I know, his was a typical military family, with no big issues. Although, once I stayed over with him for a couple of days around New Year's and it was clear that his mom tended to drink a little bit beyond social.

James always stood out. Classically handsome, he dressed unusually well even when he was of college age. Now when we get together, he is dressed in Cuccinelli tropical weight suits with handmade shoes and expensive ties. He is the kind of guy that everyone notices when he enters a room. It is no exaggeration to say movie-star appearance. Tall, silver-haired, still very fit, his expensive gold-rimmed glasses and luxury watch complete the picture. Even in his late fifties, I could see women checking him out when we went out to dinner.

More significantly, he was always a risk taker – driving too fast, skiing too fast – generally up for just about anything. He is always the dominant alpha character in any group setting.

For James, joining the military seemed almost automatic. His role model was his dad, and his older brother was also an officer. He was into the army in his head before he came to the college.

Everybody had their different baggage and skills that they brought with them to RMC. In James' case it was hockey. He was a seriously good hockey player, maybe NHL good. Unfortunately, he had a habit of taking cheap shots at opponents, hitting them out of the ref's view, which turned off any scouts. Hey, that kind of colouring outside the lines might even be the defining feature of James. It certainly was an element of his life after the army.

Speaking of the army, the three of us did infantry school together. The other two stayed infantry. I switched to the air force after phase one of infantry school. Something about camping out in the dirt didn't work for me. My dad used to joke that he came to Canada so he could crap indoors.

While the three of us were in the services after graduation, it was easy to keep in touch. James and Mato both ended up at PPCLI in Edmonton. James even got married there, although it fell apart within three years. He has a daughter somewhere from that time.

Before he left the army, James' last posting was to Namibia as part of the UN Transition Assistance Group – peacekeepers, separating the South Africans from SWAPO during withdrawal and elections. That was his first intro to Africa and something must have clicked, because he has been there on and off ever since.

We lost track of him for a while. After the UN tour, he left the army and vanished. I saw him infrequently and he was never open about what he was up to. There were rumours that he was serving as a mercenary somewhere in Africa, but when I asked what he was up to he always changed the subject. He gave off a vibe that he didn't want to talk about it.

In 2002, James set up his own business, JaMAC, specializing in the weapons trade. Apparently, the mercenary work had given him a network of contacts that he could use to build his own empire. As might be expected, most of that trade is in Africa. He seemed to mostly operate in Nairobi, and finally in Doadja.

The arms trade must be very lucrative, because James normally travels by private jet and I know that he owns a home on Mustique, that luxe island for the ultra-wealthy in the Caribbean. He also has an apartment in Amsterdam and a condo in Yorkville in Toronto. Otherwise, I guess he must have a home in Doadja, but when he is anywhere else, he simply stays in luxury hotels.

Mato and I have led much more conventional lives since graduation from RMC. Matt Hawney was a completely bilingual anglophone when I met him. He grew up in Moncton, New Brunswick. I'm not sure how he ended up going to RMC, because his family had no interest in the military at all. Maybe it was the outdoors thing. His family is big on camping, canoeing, fishing, hunting, and outdoors survival activities. Matt was a good fit for the army. He joined the army cadets in Moncton at sixteen, and then went to cadet camps for a couple of summers, so he knew the army well.

That bit of army background and the fact that he was an ace soccer player who excelled academically is what got RMC interested in him. Oh, yes, he also plays a mean twelve-string guitar.

Like James, Matt stayed in the infantry. He was posted to the PPCLI with James, and then moved to other postings in Germany, in various places with the UN, and then to Ottawa, where he got his M.Sc. in Computer science.

I'm not sure what triggered his move out of the army. Maybe it was the weaknesses caused by lack of investment in the military, or maybe he was recruited by the Communications Security Establishment (CSE). Anyway, he moved from DND to CSE where he is now leader of the information warfare protection unit that defends government agencies from hacking. He is the "dad" of the group, much older than his team.

Because I am based in Ottawa, I see Mato often. Like most of my military college classmates, he has kept himself fit and is not carrying any extra weight. Of course, his hair has thinned and greyed, but otherwise he doesn't seem to have changed that much. In a town where almost nobody dresses well, anytime I meet him for lunch, he is always wearing a sharp suit and tie. His year-round outdoor time when he is not working keeps him tanned.

Our wives got to know each other, and even the kids see each other when they can. It is great having a few drinks or a meal with Matt because his work means that he is on top of world affairs. It is like drinking from a fire hose when I ask him about some nation, or some event that it is in the news.

I don't envy Matt's job. Although he loves it, it keeps him on edge. His biggest worry seems to be that the Five Eyes intelligence alliance would completely miss some shift in an area of the World. His second big concern is the lack of seriousness of the Canadian government about national security and national defence. After a couple of glasses of wine, he is scathing about the government's lack of interest in protecting Canadians and working with our allies. His perspective is that the government is now just an organization that is geared to issuing press releases. In his mind, the gap between the stated intent and reality is huge.

Matt's son Dan is an officer in JTF2, the Canadian special forces unit.

As for me, well, RMC was strangely a bit of a natural fit. You may deduce from my name, Nadeem Nawaz, that I am from an immigrant family. We came to Canada from Pakistan when I was six. The fit with RMC comes from my granddad who was an officer in the Indian Army Sixth Infantry Division. This was, of course, prior to Partition in 1947. The pride my family had in the exploits of Granddad was a constant in my youth. The other thing that drove me toward military service was the appreciation of the opportunities that Canada had enabled my family to have, opportunities that my parents really grabbed onto. Dad was an entrepreneurial mechanical engineer, and by the time I was in my teens, we were living in the tony Point Grey area of Vancouver and I went to Lord Byng High.

Well, it was the seventies when I was of high school age. Even though Vancouver then was becoming cosmopolitan, Point Grey was whitey white. There were a few Chinese-Canadian kids in the school, but I was the only Desi. Naturally, there were some racist issues, but I just tried to move on and fit in. Rugby was my serious sport, and we had an excellent team at that high school, so that helped me connect.

RMC was a blast for me. I loved the camaraderie at the college and during summer training. I still have memories burned into my brain from infantry school at the end of first year. Now when I read a novel that has time slowing down during some adventurous action, I know it can be true. One time, James and I were doing an escape and evasion seventy-two-hour trek. On the second night, after hours of darkness, we were leopard-crawling past a sentry post when James triggered a trip flare. Jeez, the time between when I heard what seemed like an amazingly loud sound of the spoon triggering the flare and the burst of light seemed like about twenty seconds. In reality, it was one ono-second (as in, Oh, no!). I can still hear that exact ping, and smell the flare, all these years later.

After college, while I kept in touch with the RMC gang and served with several of my closest friends, I left the military once my obligatory service was completed. It just didn't grab me that much. I managed to get a Master's degree in political science before I finished my military time and aced the foreign service officer's entry tests, so I became a diplomat. Global Affairs Canada loved the fact that I spoke English, French, Urdu, Pashto, and Punjabi. I have since spent my whole career at Global Affairs, until very recently when I moved to the Prime Minister's Office (PMO) as Chief Security Advisor.

Like the others, I have aged, of course, and am not as fit as James and Matt are now, but I have kept myself together and am only ten kilos heavier than I was in college. I like to think if you saw me on the street or in a social setting, you would be thinking, diplomat or university professor.

My daughter, Alida, also went to RMC and was in the same class as Dan, Matt's son. Those two are close. Alida left the military after six years, including a tour in Afghanistan. Even though she only served six years, I was proud that she chose RMC and it seems to have served her well. For a young woman, the military college experience can build a self-confidence that is hard to match. When she graduated, she knew that she was physically and mentally strong and ready to compete in any environment. She is a rising star in the private sector.

Given the situation with James, it seemed that if we were going to help, it needed immediate action, so I emailed Matt to propose lunch in the bar at Ottawa's Rideau Club the next day. Matt likes the club. We would spend more time together there, but Matt's wife finds it a bit too dressed-up and stuffy. She is more of a jeans and burgers person.

I went to the club a bit early to get a table in the bar and waited for Matt. As expected, he showed up on time.

"Mato, good to see you, man. How's the family?"

"Good, what about you? I haven't seen Alida in ages, is she doing well?"

"I can't remember if I told you, but KPMG has moved her into forensic accounting and she loves that. Digging out fraud suits her."

"I can see that. She always had a powerful sense of right and wrong, and attention to detail."

"In any case, Matt, right now we are all doing better than James."

"True, Nadeem, but nothing surprises me with James, he always pushed the limits. I do want to help him, though. We have been through some amazing times together."

"Yes, he is a crazy guy, but also smart. Hard to believe that he would do something that would get him locked up. Let's order lunch before we really get into this."

To get started, Matt ordered a craft beer and I opted for a glass of chardonnay. We waited until we were served before continuing.

"Matt, since we got the email from Sabi, I did a bit of superficial digging using Global Affairs sources, and I can confirm that the situation is bad. Regardless of what James has been imprisoned for, and there may be no reason at all, it is bad. The country is a shithole, the president has absolute power, there is no rule of law, and the prison is one of the worst in the world."

"Okay, but other than that?" Mato smiled.

"Yeah, right, other than that."

"Any ideas, Nadeem?"

"Well, Matt, I think the sensible starting point must be diplomatic or semi-diplomatic. I can make inquiries and make it seem like official Canadian government business. In fact, it can be official – there is a Canadian citizen in prison, we need to know why, what the course of justice is, etc."

"What about bribery or ransom money, Nadeem? My impression is that in a country like that, bribery goes a long way."

"That is certainly an option to explore."

We talked a bit more about our history with James, then ordered lunch.

"Mr. Nawaz, what can I bring for you and your friend?

Matt jumped in.

"I will have the chowder and the salmon, please."

"And for you, Mr. Nawaz?

"I will have the club salad and the turkey sandwich, please."

"Of course, it won't be long."

When the server had moved away, I went back to the Doadja situation.

"Matt, I think I will go to Doadja on my own account. We owe James the best effort possible. While I can make official inquiries from here, Doadjan officials may not even deign to answer. Canada is nothing to them. Also, I need to talk to this Sabi Issa directly to get a better picture. If bribery is an option, that can only be discussed off the record, in-person."

"So, in the case of bribery Nadeem, what would be talking about – the prison guards, the president, somebody else?"

"I have no idea at this point, Matt. That is something I need to explore. If it looks feasible and the amounts are sensible, then we can round up old classmates and try to put together what we need."

We finished lunch. I told Matt that I would book a flight to Doadja and use my drag to try and meet with senior officials, even the President, if possible, and spend time with Sabi Issa.

"I am going to start here first, pushing official inquiries through whatever mission has responsibility for Canada's interests in Doadja. If that turns out to be fruitless, then I will go there and fill you in as soon as I get back."

I knew so little about Doadja that I had to first find out which of our embassies or high commissions looked after Doadja issues. I knew we didn't have an embassy there. It turned out to be the responsibility of the mission in Dakar, Senegal.

I sent a message to the Ambassador in Dakar.

There is a Canadian citizen, James Mackenzie, imprisoned in Doadja since January this year. No other information and inquiries on site have turned up a reason, no known potential trial. Can you make an official inquiry and let me know if you get a response?

Four days later, the response came, and it was what I expected.

Inquiries with the government of Doadja have been met with no response. We know that the messages were received. You can assume that the lack of response is a choice on the part of the government there.

I called Matt: "Let's get together at the end of the day, and I will bring you up to date on James. How about the Clocktower pub on Beechwood? I believe it's on your way home."

I got there before Matt and ordered a couple of brit-style bitters. I knew he liked those. He arrived a few minutes later.

"Nadeem, I see you are already into the beer."

"Sure, I even bought you one. I seem to remember doing that frequently during college days."

"Geez, do you remember when we paid for that keg in the mess and the whole gang got into it?"

"Hard to forget. When I think about that evening, I realize how lucky we were that nobody got injured doing that "carrier landing" thing. Flinging someone off a table into a pile of cushions while they try to light a match in the air is really ridiculous, in retrospect."

"Yeah, mostly we were landing flat on the pile, but it would have been easy to be head-down and really screw up your head or back."

"Well, we survived, and it was a lot of laughs at the time."

"It is amazing what happens at the age when you feel immortal. No doubt, the liquid courage helped a bit. We were warriors."

"Anything to eat?"

"No, I should get caught up on James, then head home. "

"Okay, Matt, here's the update. The government in Doadja is not even responding to our official inquiries. I was afraid that might happen. This is not a normal country. I think the only option is for me to go there. A personal visit might stir the government there, but in any case, I will be able to find out more about the situation from James' partner and from talking to the government officials. I will try to get to see this President Obissey."

"Any risk to you?"

"I don't think so. Jailing a resident is one thing. Interfering with a foreign government official that is simply visiting would be a whole other level."

"When can you go, Nadeem?"

"I need a couple of days to arrange to be away and to set up the trip. I'll probably leave in a few days. I won't try to email you while I am there, but let's get together again as soon as I return. I should only be there a couple of days."

Matt raised his beer in a toast.

"Good luck to you, man. See you when you get back."

Chapter 4.
Nadeem - February

The following week, I flew to Doadja, routing through Frankfurt. I had sent Sabi an email before the trip, giving him my flight details, and in case emails were monitored, indicating that I was coming to see how the Canadian government could help James' firm. Of course, this really didn't have any kind of official blessing, as I was taking a vacation to go there.

Arrival in Doadja has to be at the bottom of any traveller's bucket list. The ancient terminal is far too small to deal with the load of a wide-body aircraft, and the bureaucratic procedures are painful. A line-up snaked from the parked aircraft to the terminal entrance. Even in a pleasant location it would be annoying, but here in Doadja with its damp heat and flies, it was nasty. After twenty hours of flying, or waiting in Frankfurt, standing there, dripping sweat in the full sun, was a new low. But the line inched forward, and once inside the reason for that was clear. In front of a small counter that could handle four passengers at most, an immigration officer was handing out paper forms to fill out. Every passenger, including returning locals, had to complete the form and hand it to another officer before proceeding to the tiny baggage claim area.

By the time I arrived in the baggage claim hall, it was crammed with passengers and baggage. Not to mention, a bunch of uniformed, thuggish looking guys with automatic weapons. The racetrack baggage unit was also undersized, it was probably built to suit the first B707s, so bags were being dumped off onto the floor. The air was humid, and it seemed as hot in the terminal as it was outside.

Of course, the bureaucratic misery wasn't over. There was another large queue at the customs counters that everyone had to pass through to exit. The customs officers had a menacing air and pawed randomly through passenger luggage. Their approach was surprisingly direct for Westerners to deal with.

"Give me twenty dollars."

"No, why would I do that?"

"So that I will let you pass. It is nothing to you."

"It is not nothing to me, and I am not giving you twenty dollars."

"Okay, go on your way, then."

Outside the bag hall, there was a hoard of greeters, and more taxi touts, many with signs indicating for whom they were looking. I assumed Sabi would have a sign with my name on it, then finally there he was, a middle-aged, tall, and slender Doadjan with a welcoming smile. Because almost all people in the crowd were slender, the only unique feature of Sabi was a whitish scar across his upper neck, on the right side.

"Sabi, I'm Nadeem."

Shaking my hand, he responded;

"Hello, Nadeem, have you got all your luggage? Good, then let's get out of here."

We weaved across the road in front of the terminal to a parking lot. Dodging car-size potholes filled with filthy water, we worked our way over to the SUV and driver that Sabi had waiting.

"Let me take you to your hotel, Nadeem. Unfortunately, there is only one okay hotel in the city, the Continental."

"Sounds okay."

"Not really. Clean enough, is all I can say. Don't leave your toothbrush out when you are not in the room. People here are extremely poor, lacking even the basics. The cleaning staff may take advantage of access to a toothbrush to give their own teeth a cleaning. Oh, and don't use the pool, even if it looks okay," he warned.

We drove ten minutes into town, pulling up in front of the mold-stained plaster façade of the hotel.

"What's the plan, Sabi?"

"I will pick you up in the morning and take you to our offices where we can discuss what can be done to get James out."

"What time?"

"I will be here at eight-thirty, okay?"

"Right, see you tomorrow, Sabi. Thanks for meeting me."

Tuesday morning, the hotel's continental breakfast was a laugh. A glass of canned orange juice and a sealed package of dry biscuits. Sabi showed up right on time. As we drove through the slow downtown traffic Sabi said, "I have to get some cash," and started texting each time traffic came to a stop. As we were passing a local bank, a boy about twelve or thirteen ran out between the cars and tapped on Sabi's window. Rolling down the window, Sabi grabbed a handful of bills.

"What was that?"

"A Doadja ATM," laughed Sabi.

We pulled into a large compound where several military vehicles were parked, mostly old Russian BMPs. The compound had a two-storey warehouse in the middle. It was quite large compared with other buildings I had seen in Doadja. Sabi led me inside. The ground floor of the warehouse was an arms depot. Stacks of wooden crates with black lettering like M136 AT4 were everywhere. More vehicles were parked inside as well. The second storey of the warehouse had a large area that was being used for additional storage – helmets, vests, and more crates of light weapons. Part of this floor had enclosed offices, and Sabi took me past a reception area into one of the offices.

"Coffee?"

"Sure, thanks, Sabi."

"Jeanine, please bring a coffee for Nadeem and me."

When the coffee arrived, we sat down at opposite sides of an old wooden desk. Sabi briefed me on the situation.

"Nadeem, let me recap what I tried to sum up in my email to you. There has been no change in James' situation, and he is still in prison. Prisons here are unbelievably bad. Very few people are released, and it is common knowledge that conditions are extremely inhumane, with disease, starvation, and dehydration all playing a role in numerous deaths."

"Since I emailed you, I haven't made much progress. I have called the President's office several times, asking for the Chief of Staff, but he doesn't take or return my calls. I don't know much more than what I passed to you before. You might have more luck as a foreigner."

I responded uncertainly.

"I did initiate an official inquiry from the Canadian government, but no response came from Doadja, so being a foreigner isn't likely to be of much help. I can try to call the President's office, but you should know that I have to be cautious. I can imply that I am here officially as a rep of the Canadian government, but if asked directly, I will have to say that I am here in a personal role."

"Still, it's worth a try. We need to find out what caused the problem with the President. Without knowing the cause, it is hard to propose solutions."

"Can you put a call through to the office of the President, then give me the phone?"

Sabi dialed and handed me the phone.

"Office of the President," said a voice on the line.

"Good morning, this is Nadeem Nawaz of the office of the Prime Minister of Canada. I am in Doadja on business and would like a brief meeting with the President, or his Chief of Staff."

"One moment, please."

Several minutes later,

"I am sorry, there is no one available currently. Can I call you back?"

"Certainly, I am at JaMAC and you can reach me at the office of Sabi Issa."

"Fine."

"Sabi, is there anything more we can do while we wait to hear back?

"Not that I can think of."

"A question; is bribery a possible way of getting James released?" I asked.

Sabi explained, "If we were dealing with some local official, it might be possible, because there is a lot of low-level bribery here. However, dealing with the President is a completely different story. In reality, we are already bribing him on a scale of tens of millions of dollars each year, as a result of him forcing himself into a fifty percent share of net income from JaMAC's arms sales. Also, he is already one of the wealthiest people in the world. No doubt, you saw some of the deplorable conditions that exist in Doadja as you came into town. The people here are just scraping by. But the country has a lot of oil. The President's father treated the national oil revenue as his personal income, and the current guy has simply followed in his footsteps. He is worth billions, has properties in Chelsea, on the Côte d'Azur, and in Cape Town. He has a Gulfstream G800 jet at the airport. This guy cannot be bribed except on a scale beyond your imagination."

"What about the Chief of Staff?" I asked.

"No, Austin is completely loyal to the President and would also be risking his life to go against him in any way. That applies to other possible targets as well, like the commandant of the prison. The problem is that everyone here knows about James. He is possibly the only white guy in the prison. Springing him would immediately be known to everyone, including the President. I would say that bribery is an unlikely route. The direct involvement of an outsider like you may be a more successful approach," advised Sabi.

"I guess I will just wander around getting to know the city while we wait to hear back."

"Don't do that," warned Sabi, "there is a high crime rate in town, even in daylight. Nighttime is dangerous, even without being mugged. Thieves regularly steal the manhole covers in the sidewalks and we have incidents of people falling in when it's dark. I will arrange for a car and driver to show you around and he will be available to take you somewhere for dinner each night. I will have the driver come to your hotel at nine tomorrow morning.

"Thanks for the heads-up," I said.

"Tonight, I will pick you up for dinner. Let me drive you back now."

Sabi took me back to the hotel.

"Pick you up at seven, Nadeem, see you later."

At seven sharp, the SUV pulled up with Sabi and another person in the front. I hopped in the back. The person riding shotgun was in a mix of camo pants and a well-worn Hawaiian shirt.

"Nadeem, this is Adam, our gunner."

"Excuse me?"

"Ha, I thought that would make you jump. We are going to a roadside grill along the highway. Night here can be edgy, so we take our own bodyguard."

Adam turned around and smiled. I could see that he had an AK47 on his lap. Yikes.

We pulled up to an area of patio tables, and behind that was a series of grills made from half-cut old oil barrels. A cloud of smoke wafted across the highway. Basic, but it smelled good. Cooking on the grills were varying sizes of beef chunks, along with spatchcocked chickens. The chicken looked great, the beef less so. The beef looked like it had been butchered with a bush knife. Pieces appeared to be three cm thick on one end, and one cm thick on the other. We ordered a couple of local beers, then the grill man came by:

"Chicken or beef?"

"Chicken for me," said Sabi.

"Same for me."

"Why no beef, it is real cow beef tonight," asked our server.

"No, thanks, chicken looks good," replied Sabi.

I waited until the server had walked away.

"Sabi, what did he mean by real cow beef?"

"Well, here the local approach is that all red meat, any meat that isn't chicken or fish, is called beef, including bush meat. People order beef here without even asking what it is sometimes."

Anyway, the chicken was good, very spicy, full of flavour, and the local beer was fine. Sabi paid, and as near as I could tell, dinner cost about four dollars for both of us.

Wednesday morning, the car was there, as promised. A bit of a beater, an old Corolla, but the driver spoke some English.

"Mr. Nawaz?"

"Yes, hello."

"I am Samson, your driver."

Samson looked like many of the other locals I had seen since arrival. Extremely thin, even hungry-looking, middle-aged with salt and pepper hair and a matching beard. Well-used jeans, rubber sandals, and a faded T-shirt that read Maggie's Revenge Roppongi completed the Doadja look.

"Okay, Samson, the plan is to show me the city. I have lots of time. I would like to see all the areas – the palace, the wealthy areas, the poor areas, the prison, the port, the airport."

"No problem, Mr. Nawaz. Sometimes it will be slow, the traffic can be bad."

"Understood. Please just call me Nadeem."

We headed off, in the order that I mentioned, starting at the palace. Although it was in the middle of the old city, the palace itself was not a colonial legacy. An ostentatious, large building surrounded by concrete walls, it looked like it was twenty or thirty years old. I imagine it was classy inside, but because of the heat and humidity, the outer walls were stained with black mold.

There was an inner courtyard in front of the palace, contained within the walls. I could see it through the gate area. The gate had a modern looking gatehouse with several paramilitary looking guys inside, and four more patrolling with automatic weapons in front of the gate.

After the palace, we continued to an area that must be the upper-class district. It was quite pleasant; in a forested area. Although the area wasn't large, it had several sizeable homes, each with a surrounding wall.

"Who lives here, Samson?"

"Mostly government officials, the big men. The head of the army, the president's chiefs, the head of the Presidential Guard, and a few oil people."

"A bit different from the common folk."

"Indeed, sir."

Next, we headed into the densest part of the city, with crowded shacks, unpaved roads, and open sewer ditches. As soon as traffic slowed, we were surrounded by vendors selling everything imaginable: electric fans, toys, live chickens, and cooked food. As soon as they saw a foreigner in the car, the crowd of vendors swelled. Mixed in with the merchants were assorted beggars, pressing sick children or severed limbs against our car window. It was a claustrophobic and unpleasant reminder of the disparities in this nasty country.

"Let's go down to the waterfront and see the port and the old colonial areas."

"Okay, sir."

I thought that there might be some quaint old colonial buildings along the waterfront, but it was neither quaint nor even colonial-looking, except for the monumental prison building on the island near the waterfront.

As we approached the port area, abandoned containers were strewn about everywhere. Every piece of unbuilt ground was littered with sea containers.

"Are there always containers everywhere like this?"

"Yes, sir, Doadja doesn't export much other than oil. The containers just get abandoned here. They arrived here with cargo but there was nothing to ship back out. It gets worse every year."

The waterfront itself was a confused mixture of older port elements, with some old warehouses, ancient derelict cranes, mixed in with newer, but poorly maintained container cranes and related equipment.

The ocean itself was littered with plastic debris, jammed in among the wharves. Bottles, plastic bags, and discarded plastic toys appeared to be in deep layers in the blackened water. A sheen of oil covered the open areas further out.

"Samson, tell me about the prison."

"It was originally a slave prison, sir. Arab traders and warring tribes would bring captives down to the city from far inland, even beyond Doadja, into the interior of the continent, to trade with the colonists. Sometimes there were vast numbers of slaves. The prison was built to assemble and hold the slaves until ships could take them to the Americas."

"And today?"

"It continued to be used as a prison by the colonial authorities until the country was liberated in 1968. For a few years after that, it was abandoned, but then our government determined a need for a place to hold criminals, so a small part of it was reopened."

"What kind of criminals?"

"You know, the usual. Murderers, thieves, rapists."

"Any political prisoners?"

"Oh, I would know nothing about that, sir."

"What about the rest of the prison island, it is a very large castle-like building?"

"Well, the part closest to the city side of the island is the base for One Battalion of our army."

"When you say base, do you mean that they train there, and are there during the day, or do they actually live there?"

"Everything, sir – live, eat, train, store their equipment."

"Wow, the soldiers live in part of the old prison?"

"Yes, sir, I believe it isn't very nice, so the officers don't live there, but the soldiers don't have any choice."

"No choice? I take it they aren't volunteers?"

"That's right, sir, we have conscription here for the army. If you are selected, you must serve three years. Marriage isn't allowed for those that are conscripted while they serve, so the men are all single. Any volunteers are in the air force or the Presidential Guard."

"How does conscription work here?"

"I would say, there are no rules. Maybe there are somewhere, but it is a matter of luck. Members of the president's tribe are luckier than others, so there are fewer of them that are sent to the army."

"How big is the army?"

"We have One Battalion here, then Two Battalion in the south about two hundred km away in Bafala, and Three Battalion on the eastern border in Kaldo. Each battalion is about six hundred soldiers, I think."

"And what about the navy?"

"Conscripted, sir, but small. We have two patrol boats here and two more in the south."

"The air force?"

"You will see it at the airport, sir. Two fighters, one cargo plane. The air force also looks after the presidential plane."

"Let's go out to the airport. I came in through there only a couple of days ago but was tired from a long flight and didn't see that much."

"Right, sir."

The drive to the airport reminded me of other African suburban drives, except with more plastic garbage blowing around. A strip of roadside bars, shops, and small open-air restaurants lined the route. Between the edge of the highway and the front of these buildings, a dusty, worn path served an endless line of pedestrians, many carrying loads. Loads on their head, loads on pushed bicycles, loads on pulled handcarts.

The airport was no more impressive on second viewing than it was on the first. The single storey concrete terminal building was painted powder blue, and bore a large sign that read, "Obissey International Airport." Every building, including the control tower adjacent to the terminal, was painted that same colour, and had the same tired look of needing a new coat of paint.

The airport fire hall was not a confidence builder. The crash-fire-rescue trucks were parked in the open in front of the hall, but half-metre-long grass surrounded the vehicles, one of which had flat tires, and the other which had a goat tied to the bumper.

A hangar standing off some distance to the right of the terminal housed two fighter jets. They were clearly Russian-made planes, but I wasn't close enough, or up to date enough on Russian aircraft, to determine the model.

Nothing about the airport looked maintained. The apron in front of and next to the terminal building had endured so many years of fuel spills and/or hydraulic leaks that it looked like the asphalt had turned into a viscous, semi-liquid mush. The ground handling equipment was in disarray. Even the runway was rutted and damaged from years without maintenance.

The far side of the airfield was littered with aircraft of varying sizes, mostly freighters of some sort.

"What are those aircraft doing, Samson?"

"They have been here for years, sir. They are abandoned. For many years, we had UN food flights running into the interior. When that stopped, these aircraft were just left here."

"Okay, Samson, that's it for today. Please take me back to the Continental."

"Yes, sir, do you want me to take you to someplace for dinner later?"

"Please, Mr. Issa tells me that the hotel is not a good choice."

"Oh, no, sir, no one would want to eat there!"

"Are there some better options?"

"Yes, the oil people have money to spend when they come and go, and of course the government leaders dine out frequently with guests."

"Come back at seven. Is that a suitable time for dinner here?

"Yes, sir, seven it is."

Samson was right on time, already waiting outside the hotel when I went down. He drove me south, out of town, along the coast and about ten klicks out. We arrived at a strip of modern-looking restaurants, bars, and nightclubs along the water. Many had waterfront patios.

He dropped me off in front of a restaurant called *Club Nautique*. A kind of doorman *cum* security guard, with a large nightstick in his belt, rushed out to open my door.

Inside, we could have been in Miami Beach. Not just the décor, but the crowd and the money. Some tables had bottles of Johnny Walker Black, or Christal champagne on them. At a long, attractive bar, three bartenders were making exotic-looking mixed drinks.

The patrons were straight out of a *Star Wars* bar scene. There was a mix of high-income young locals sporting heavy bling, and some serious looking UN types in the usual multi-pocket safari vests. There were also a few thuggish-looking Russian guys, and some high-roller types in tropical suits from the oil industry. Naturally, the usual contingent of local prostitutes was working the crowd.

The real shocker, though, was the prices. Higher than Miami! Really astounding when you consider that most of the country was having trouble finding enough to eat. Although, I have no doubt that the clientele here could well afford it. The menu included many items that were clearly flown in daily – *Fines de Claire* oysters, Nova Scotia lobster, Wagyu beef, and New Zealand

Lamb. The only local items were fish. I selected simple, going with local fish and a glass of Chablis.

Samson picked me up later that evening and took me back to the hotel.

"What is the plan for tomorrow, sir?"

"Pick me up at nine in the morning and take me to Sabi's office, please. Goodnight."

At the JaMAC offices on Thursday, there was nothing to do but read and poke around on the Web. It seemed wise to assume that, in a country like this, all electronic correspondence may be monitored, so I didn't want to communicate with Matt or my office from here.

Finally, on Thursday afternoon, there was a call back from the president's office, indicating that the Chief of Staff would meet with me on Monday at one-thirty. This was painfully slow; it had taken a week to get my first meeting.

On the way back to the hotel, I asked Samson, "Is there anything else that I should see?"

"Some visitors go to see the national park."

"Tell me about it."

"It isn't far, it starts just on the edge of the city and stretches forty km to the eastern border. There is a network of dirt roads. There is a chance to see wild animals and there are some tiny cottages near waterholes for rent."

"Okay, I'm not going to accomplish anything in town this weekend. Please book us two of those cottages and take me out there to explore. What about food?"

"Absolutely, sir. I will bring food and you can pay me for the food and the cabins later. I can cook, too."

"Bring enough beer for both of us as well, Samson."

"And tomorrow, sir?

"I am just going to work at the hotel. Pick me up Saturday morning at nine."

"Okay, Mr. Nadeem."

Friday, I read for a while, and looked up whatever I could find on the Web about Doadja and Obissey. It didn't look like the country had the skilled expertise to censor the Web, so I found out quite a bit, some of it not very flattering. There was nothing good to say about the country. There is no rule of law, there are many political prisoners, and it has one of the worst jails on the face of the earth with high rates of prisoner fatalities. Doadja is ruled by a "president for life" who treats the national wealth as his own personal piggy bank.

In terms of national indicators, Doadja is:

- The country's GDP per capita is surprisingly high at nine thousand dollars. However, this average is misleading because it includes the oil wealth, which mostly falls into the hands of Obissey personally. The most common salary level is equivalent to about thirty Canadian dollars per year.

- In terms of human rights, the country is close to the bottom in world rankings, with reports of, "murders of civilians by the Presidential Guard, kidnappings by government agencies, arbitrary arrests, torture of prisoners, life-threatening conditions in prisons, trafficking of women and children for commercial sexual exploitation, illegal weapons trading, and violence against minority tribal groups."

- The UN reports that ten percent of Doadjan children do not make it to the age of five, and sixty percent of the population does not have access to clean drinking water.

- With respect to President Obissey:

- He was born in 1962 in a small village in Doadja and grew up there until he was a teenager. His father was an army major when he seized control of the government and moved the family into the palace in Nambi, the capital of Doadja.

- He was educated at a Catholic mission, followed by a Bachelor of Arts at some minor American college and an MBA from Temple University in the USA.

- He remained in the US for four years after university until his father became ill, when he returned home and quickly stepped into the presidency. There was some opposition to this in-family transition, but he quickly and violently suppressed it.

- All the photos online indicate that he is shorter than average. He typically wears a suit and tie, except for ceremonial occasions, where he shows up in a gilded version of the national dress, a powder blue robe with gold animals embroidered on it.

- He is reported to suffer from a variety of health issues, including heart disease, obesity, and gout. The gout may explain his slow walk and limp, which is noticeable in some of the news clips online.

- He speaks Doadjan, English (with a French accent), French, and some Spanish.

- He appears to be a serious fellow. None of the news clips show him gesturing or smiling. He looks ominous in most of them.

- His wife, Angela, is a powerful figure in her own right. A big shopper, she spends months each year in Europe at their properties in France, the UK, and Spain. Obissey himself spends less time out of the country, jetting back and forth without notice, possibly due to concern over a coup in his absence.

- He reportedly frequently has a mistress at the palace, but these are short-term positions.

- His friends and supporters include:
  - Austin Mbaye – his Chief of Staff, who has been with him for years.

- General Henri Yalumba – the head of the Army.
- Colonel Jacob Obissey – his cousin, who is head of the Presidential Guard.

- He does not have broad support from the population, but his rule is viewed as unchangeable by most. From time to time there have been small rebellions, but they were ruthlessly put down. There have been none of those in the last four years. Several leadership alternatives are in exile.

- In dealings with the outside world, he retains a Washington public relations firm that constantly tries to polish his image as "a friend of the west," etc. Other countries are well aware of the appalling education levels, poverty, human rights abuses, and criminal activities. They are also aware that the country is a key distribution point for the drug trade into Europe, as well as human trafficking.

Like several other adjacent countries, things are so bad in Doadja that it is surprising that there has not been a national uprising. Forty years of oppression, theft, and corruption has made the population believe that what they are experiencing is a normal state of affairs.

· · · · · · · · · ·

Saturday, Samson picked me up as planned.

"Samson, you say the park isn't far?"

"Not far at all, sir. It starts just at the city edge. The lodge is well into the park and the roads are not really roads, so it will take us about an hour and half from the edge of the park to the cabins."

"What will we see?"

"Possibly chimps, leopards, cape buffalo, elephants, hippos, and crocodiles. There are also many snakes, but we will try to avoid those. To see the most, we will take the car out early in the morning at dawn and again at sunset. During the day it is much more difficult to see the animals. I suggest tomorrow after the morning game drive we get a guide and walk to where we might see the gorillas."

Not really roads, really summed it up. In many areas the bush had encroached on the road and I could hear the Stay-a-While thorns scraping the paint off the car. We weren't far into the forest when there were large yellow and black spiders on thick pale green webs running across the road. We started to drive into them, breaking the webs, and some of these nasty-looking giants landed on the windshield.

"Jesus, what are those? Are they dangerous?"

"No, sir, not dangerous. They are Golden Orb spiders, and this is the peak time of year for them. They are harmless."

"I still wouldn't want to run into one when we are walking to see the gorillas. They are scary."

"The guide will be in front of us, sir. No worries."

We arrived at the cabins shortly before lunch. They were very modest. White plaster, and quite small, with thatched roofs. Samson prepared us some spicy noodles for lunch. Then we read until sundown, when we opened a bottle of duty-free gin that I had brought and sat out on the deck.

"It is time to take a drive if you want, sir."

"Great, let's go."

The light was still good, but fading fast. It didn't take five minutes on the bush road until we came across a large group of baboons using the road as their path. A little while later, Samson stopped the car and quickly turned off the engine.

"Do you see that large tree about one hundred and fifty metres away just off the right side of the road? It has a termite mound just to the left of it."

"Yes."

"Look at the large branch on the right side of the tree, below the heavy canopy."

"What am I looking for?"

"There is a leopard laying on that branch."

"Wow, good eyes! In this light it is hard to pick out, but now that you have pointed it out, I can see it clearly."

"You are lucky, Mr. Nadeem. I have been here many times and have only seen a leopard twice. The light is fading, let's continue."

After about half a kilometre, we came to a low spot where the road entered a pool of water. On the far side of the pool, a bull elephant stared across at us.

"We will wait, sir, to see if he moves on. I do not wish to get closer."

"No problem."

Samson left the engine running in case we needed to back up in a hurry, but nothing exciting happened, nor did the big elephant move.

"It is getting dark. I am going to back up and take you back to the cabins."

"Fine, this has been great. It has been some years since I was last on a bush drive."

"You have done bush drives before, sir?"

"Yes, Samson, I have spent some years in Africa working and have gone on safari in Rwanda, Kenya, and Botswana. It is a good experience every time."

"You may have seen more animals in other countries, sir. Here, the poor people sometimes enter the park and take animals for bushmeat."

Sunday morning, Samson knocked on my cabin door around five-thirty, carrying a pot of tea.

"Good morning, we will leave in twenty minutes. My plan is to go east to a large waterhole and lake area where we will catch the animals and see the water creatures – the hippos and crocs. By the way, that area is also completely full of birds, if you have any interest in birds. The guide will meet us there, and we will follow him in his vehicle to the jumping-off point to hike uphill to where we might see the gorillas."

"Excellent plan, Samson."

Everything unfolded as planned. We saw a complete list of animals around the ponds, including the less famous warthogs and jackals. There was an extended family of hippos in one large pool. We met up with the guide and drove for about forty minutes into an area of dense jungle, and then proceeded on foot. As I had hoped, we did manage to find a gorilla family. We just stood there and observed for about a half-hour, without speaking, then turned and returned to the car.

"Samson, that was amazing. It was obvious that the gorillas knew we were there, but after a couple of minutes, they just ignored us and went about their normal life."

Sunday afternoon, Samson dropped me back in town.

· · · · · · · · · ·

Monday, Samson picked me up at one and dropped me off at the palace gate.

"I will park the car and wait across the road in the restaurant where I can see you when you come out."

"Okay, thank you."

At the palace gatehouse, Presidential Guard staff took me through a procedure to check if I had an appointment. They required me to leave my cell phone in a box, and then walk through a metal detector. One of the guards then took me across the courtyard into the palace building. He led me to an anteroom and told me to sit.

Shortly after one-thirty, a staffer came out of one of the many doors to the seating area.

"Mr. Nawaz?"

"Yes."

"Come with me, please."

She led me to an office and announced my presence as she opened the door.

"Mr. Nawaz is here to see you, sir."

A well-dressed, middle-aged man stood and pointed me to the seat opposite his desk. With his suit and tie, and heavy, black-rimmed glasses, he definitely looked like a leading bureaucrat.

"Mr. Nawaz, I am Austin Mbaye, the Chief of Staff to the President. How can I help you?"

His English was perfect, upper-class Brit. Probably UK-educated.

"Mr. Mbaye, I am here to make inquiries about James Mackenzie, a Canadian citizen currently being detained in the Wailing Island prison, I believe. My interest is in what Mr. Mackenzie has been charged with, what the procedures are in Doadja to bring him to trial, under what conditions he would be granted bail, and if there is anything that I can do to speed resolution of this case."

"Mr. Nawaz, an experienced diplomat such as yourself would surely know that the procedures here are very dissimilar to what you might expect in Canada. I can only advise you that we took Mr. Mackenzie into custody at the direction of the President. He has not been formally charged and will only be released on the orders of the President."

"Do you have any understanding of the reasons for this detention and of what would enable the President to consider his release?" I inquired.

"I can only tell you that the root issue is a commercial disagreement. Specifically, a failure of Mr. Mackenzie to comply with the terms of an agreement he has with President Obissey. I have no indication of what might encourage the President to release James Mackenzie. I can only suggest setting up a meeting for you with the President so that he can inform you of the situation."

"Thank you, could that be set up soon? I need to return to Canada as soon as possible."

He picked up the phone.

"Maria, what is the President's availability to meet with Mr. Nadeem Nawaz of the Canadian diplomatic corps? Wednesday at eleven, fine."

He turned back to me.

"Return here in time for an eleven o'clock meeting on Wednesday with the President. I will inform the gate house."

"Thank you for your help, Mr. Mbaye."

I left his office to find a Presidential Guard waiting to escort me to the gatehouse.

· · · · · · · · · ·

Tuesday was another wasted day. I had lunch with Sabi and brought him up to date on my meeting with Austin and the planned meeting with the President.

"This is not looking good. I hope that Wednesday goes better. At least you managed to get a meeting."

· · · · · · · · · ·

Wednesday, Samson dropped me back at the palace., I went through the whole cellphone and screening routine at the gate and was escorted through the palace entrance. A staffer led me to a different anteroom this time. This one was larger, with about twenty soft chairs lined up along three walls, fifteen of which were filled with a variety of locals waiting – some in suits, some in local garb. Oh, no, I had seen this "big man scene" elsewhere in Africa. I knew I was in for a long wait.

Sure enough, at a slow pace, a staffer would come into the room and call out a name, leading the selected person into the

President's office. My turn came at twelve thirty. The office was a typical African leader's office. Large, windowless, with a row of chairs around the walls facing the leader's desk. The President was behind a very large but bare desk and I was simply pointed to stand in front of the desk, with no invitation to be seated. The President was very heavy, and not at all healthy-looking. The staffer introduced me.

"Sir, I have Mr. Nadeem Nawaz of Canada to see you."

"Mr. Nawaz, what brings you to my office?"

"Mr. President, I am here to make inquiries with respect to the detention of James Mackenzie. I met with Austin Mbaye on Monday and he suggested that I meet directly with you if possible."

"What is your interest in Mr. Mackenzie?"

"I am inquiring about the next steps in terms of you bringing him to court or releasing him, and if there is anything I can do to assist the process. For example, is there a fine to be paid? Do we need to retain a lawyer?"

"Mr. Nawaz, no one in Ottawa informed me that you were coming to Doadja. Are you here in an official role on behalf of Canada?"

"No, sir, I am here as a friend of James Mackenzie."

"Just a friend, not a business associate? Do you have any personal role in JaMAC, James' company?"

"I do not."

"Very fortunate for you. Otherwise, you might be joining him in our famous prison. James defied me, violated our agreement, and disrespected me. He will get out of prison whenever I think it is time, which may be never. I am tired of white people disrespecting Doadja. I allowed James to establish his business here and to prosper. He is a multi-millionaire because of our deal. He prospered in our glorious country because I allowed him to, and then he steals from me by hiding income that he owes. He can rot in prison. That's all I have to say, good day."

He scowled and waved his hand to dismiss me as if he were swatting a fly.

Leaving the palace in the usual escorted way, I had Samson take me to see Sabi at his office.

"How did it go?"

"Couldn't be worse. He threatened to jail me if I had a holding in JaMAC, saying that James has been hiding income from him. Is that true, Sabi?"

"Only by a strange interpretation. Our contract agreement with the President specifically identifies revenue from arms sales here or abroad as the income that must be shared. We have always honoured that."

"Well, what is he pissed about, then?"

"We have other businesses that aren't part of the agreement. Maybe he thinks that they should have automatically been included in the revenue sharing deal."

"The tone was bad. I would be careful, Sabi. It sounds like he could go after you personally or after JaMAC assets. You have a lot of valuable weapons downstairs."

"Good point. What now?"

"I am going back to Canada tomorrow. I will meet with Matt and see if we can come up with any ideas that might free James. Clearly, legal actions or bribery aren't going to work. We will need to find some other solution. I'll keep you informed."

"Sabi, we need to protect our communications going forward. Do you play computer games?"

"Yes, from time to time. Why?"

"We can bury any comms within a computer game that allows messaging between the players. Do you know a game called Civilization?"

"I have heard of it; I don't have it."

"Okay, purchase a license on the Civilization website, then log on to play it every day in the late evening, say at 2200. It will be 1800 in Ottawa then. I will set up a game at my end, and then send you a test message inside the chat box in the game, so that you can locate it and message me back. That will be our communication tool for now, until we can switch to something more secure. We still need to be careful about what we say, because it isn't encrypted. It is a good cover and it looks harmless. It is unlikely to attract attention. I am going out on tomorrow's flight. I will be in touch."

"Okay, Nadeem. Let me take you out for dinner tonight. I would like to hear more about how you got involved with James. I will pick you up at six-thirty at the hotel.

Chapter 5.
Nadeem & Sabi – February

Sabi picked me up at six-thirty and took me to a small bar/restaurant on the edge of town. It was more like the first night than the places I went to on the waterfront. The clients were mostly locals, none looking very prosperous. We went up to the second floor and out onto a balcony, which was narrow and only had a couple of two-seat tables, but it was quiet and we could talk. We didn't have a bodyguard, but I noticed that Sabi had a handgun tucked in under his shirt.

We ordered some beer with fish dishes, and simply relaxed to chat. As we were talking, several women came by our table. They knew Sabi and flirted a bit before he made it clear that he was busy tonight with a guest. Later in the evening, when I tried to find the washroom and needed to walk by some "cribs" – tiny rooms, each with a single bed, I realized that the restaurant was also a brothel. A new experience for me.

Anyway, once we were served, I wanted to hear more from Sabi.

"Sabi, I see James from time to time when he comes to Canada, and I do know that he is involved in the arms trade, but it isn't something we talk about when we are together. I think it embarrasses him. I really know very little about what James has been up to since he left the army. How did you two get linked up? How did he end up here in Doadja?"

"Well, Nadeem, I was looking for a way to get out of Doadja in '92 when I finished school. I was charged-up about being in the military, but Doadja was hopeless. I looked around and there was a lot of action in other African countries. I ended up in Angola where I joined up with some mercenary fighters for about a year, but they were under-equipped and poorly led. Then the Executive Outcomes agency showed up to support the government and I was immediately attracted to them. They had it all – weapons, armour, and heli-support. I had enough field time by then that they hired me. I met James in Angola.”

“We were a tough, experienced combat crowd. When this white guy from Canada showed up to join us, we were sceptical, to say the least. We thought, ‘isn’t Canada the country where they dance around the campfire singing Kumbaya and convene peace-keeping conferences?’ So, it took a while for James to fit in, but once we saw that listened to us that had been in-theatre and that he knew what he was up to, it started to work.

I interrupted Sabi,

“That doesn’t surprise me, Sabi, one of our key, early lessons in the Canadian army was to depend on the judgement of the warrant officers and sergeants.”

Sabi continued,

“From Angola, we both moved on to Sierra Leone. That was a shitstorm as you know. The various rebel groups were just a bunch of armed, stoned teenagers. It was insanely dangerous because nothing made sense. You were as likely to be shot by a ‘friendly’ as by a group you were fighting. The whole environment was bizarre. The local idea of a contact was that all these fighters would simply go into full-automatic mode and just keep hosing down the forest with their AKs until they ran out of ammunition.”

I commented,

“Yes, I am familiar with the events in Sierra Leone. I kept current at the time and have read several books since on the wars there.”

Sabi continued,

“Let me tell you about some of the weirdness there. James and I were sent up-river to meet with a provincial governor and determine whether he was on our side or supporting one of the loony groups. The two of us went up in an old beater Russian freighter aircraft that was grossly overloaded and had a bunch of locals just sitting on the floor of the plane. When we arrived up-country, we did a circling descent to attempt to avoid being shot at as we came in on approach. At least we got there. We found the governor living in a grand old Victorian house, which had been built for the colonial governor fifty years before."

"In the middle of this ridiculous civil war, the provincial governor hosted us for lunch in a wood-panelled dining room. Various servers came and went with four courses, wine, coffee – the whole deal. After lunch, James and I went into the kitchen to thank the cooks and the kitchen was completely gutted – no stoves, no sinks, no people. But we could see the back yard from the kitchen window and there they were – the cooks, the servers – all gathered around a bonfire in the garden where they had cooked our lunch. Crazy. That was symbolic of that whole adventure. You could be in a serious firefight with a bunch of crazed fighters who believed that they couldn't be killed, and the next minute you're laughing your guts out because one of the fighters was dressed in a pink terry cloth bathrobe and an oversized cowboy hat."

"James and I were together there until '98. We spent a lot of time in firefights, in ridiculous, laughable situations, while trying to train local soldiers. By the time the mission in Sierra Leone wrapped up, James and I were tight. We trusted each other completely in bad conditions, so thereafter we moved around together."

"There was always lots to do in Africa for experienced mercenaries. We spent a while in Liberia, and some time guarding mines in the Congo. I know the perception outside Africa after Executive Outcomes wrapped up was that mercenary action was gone in Africa, but it never really stopped, right up until today."

"So how did you end up in the arms trade, Sabi?"

"By '98 James was one of the better-known Westerners in the business. The CIA was involved in arming some of the friendlies. They didn't want to have direct contact with the known arms merchants like Victor Bout or Guus Kouwenhoven, so they approached James to see if he was interested in providing weapons and ammo. That way, if things went badly, they had an out. Basically, that's how we got into the arms trade. Initially, we were just intermediaries. James would deal with Bout, arrange delivery, and take a mark-up. Almost everything was Eastern-Bloc where Bout had the contacts, but James had the link to the countries and forces being supported by the West. It worked for everyone. Even in that role, it was extremely profitable. It was also a lot of work, so James needed me, and I fit in better in local crowds as well."

"By 2000, we were making good money. But we had been risking our lives for eight years, so we decided to focus on the arms trade and stop the front-line stuff. We set up initially in Nairobi, but the atmosphere there wasn't ideal. Eventually we had to move on and it turned out that Doadja worked well, until now."

"We were in Doadja for less than six months when the President's Chief of Staff showed up at our offices and told us that President Obissey wanted to see us. James went to see him, and Obissey laid out the deal in plain terms. If we wanted to work from Doadja, Obissey insisted on being our fifty percent partner. In return, he would issue all the end-user certificates we needed to cover our business. It was perfect; with a corrupt government as a partner we didn't need to worry about a thing for years to come."

"We kept building up the arms business. With Obissey amenable to issuing end-user certificates we became even more useful to the bigger traders. On paper, Doadja was an extremely heavily-armed nation. In reality, of course, most of that firepower ended up somewhere else."

"Things really shifted into high gear in 2003 when the US jailed Bout, leaving a gaping hole in the market. By that point, James was known to the various players in Bulgaria, Romania, Russia, and Georgia that were providing weapons, so it was an easy step to move up the food chain. From then on, we were printing money."

"With the cover provided by Obissey, James was able to keep a lower profile than Bout ever had. The big dog security agencies – MI6, CIA, DGSA – all knew about James, and the UN likely did as well, but he mostly stayed out of the press. It helped that some of the high-profile wars in Africa had calmed down, and we were often supplying private military groups that were guarding mines and even some governments."

"That's the whole story. Really, we have made so much money that if James gets out of prison, he could go anywhere and live as a multi-millionaire without ever working again."

Sabi sat back and ordered more beers.

"Now it's your turn, Nadeem. Tell me how you became so close to James that you are willing to come halfway around the world to see if you can get him out of jail."

"Well, Sabi, I have known James since 1979, when we met at the Royal Military College in Canada. James and I, and a guy called Matt Hawney, ended up in the same squadron. The three of us were also at infantry school together. We not only spent the whole college year together, but also one summer in combat training. Matt and James stayed infantry for training during college and were posted together after graduation. We were so close that we visited each other's parents' homes, holidayed together, and partied together. By college grad, we were lifelong friends."

"Like your time with James, we had a lot of good times together, doing crazy shit, blowing stuff up in the summers. It was good prep for combat. We had some great experiences together that were fun but also good combat training."

"One of the training summers, we had the most insane party at a demolition site. We had rounded up some local women to join us, telling them we were having a party with fireworks. After a few beers, and lit by a couple of campfires, we set off the fireworks – a single charge of two hundred kg of C4 that was going out-of-date and needed to be disposed of. That was a sight to behold – my first mushroom cloud! Later in the evening, one of the guys attached a reel of FIB to his back and wandered through the crowd, laying the fuse down among the crowd as he chatted with people. Sometime later he set it off. It was like the whole party jumped in the air, with screams and laughter."

"Naturally, we had to do the whole drive across Canada thing together as well. Five days in the car, five nights of partying."

"After grad, we split up. James and Matt were posted to Edmonton in Western Canada and subsequently served together in Yugoslavia. It was nominally peacekeeping but was as close to combat as peacekeeping gets. That experience left them both jaded. Identical people, with the same cultural roots going at each other because one group was Catholic, another Orthodox, and the third Muslim. Anything was justified in the name of religion – women and kids were massacred, raped, and murdered. Corruption was rampant. I think that may be part of why James ended up going mercenary. He could see that UN interventions were close to useless, but mercenaries might not be."

Sabi sighed,

"Yes, anyplace where the UN has tried to bring in peacekeepers that are constrained in their ability to control the situation, it hasn't worked out well."

I continued,

"I left the military in '89, before the other two, but we stayed close. We kept in touch and got together whenever we could. You know the deal. We were really the 'band of brothers' after our time together.

"James did another tour with the UN, this time in Namibia. That may have been where he fell in love with Africa. It was after that tour that our contacts became less frequent. He left the army and went back to Africa. From what you have told me, that is when he turned up at Executive Outcomes.

"Matt stayed with the army until 2000. Then, he took a position in the Communications Security Establishment, which is part of the military. It performs electronic intelligence and prevents electronic intelligence by others. Think of it as like GCHQ in the UK or the NSA in the US, but smaller."

"And you," said Sabi, "after the army?"

"Well, I switched to the air force while I was still at military college. After I left the military, I made a successful transition to being a diplomat. I had obtained a Master's degree while serving and got accepted into our foreign affairs ministry. One of my first postings was to Kigali. That is where my fascination with Africa started. I met my wife there in the gym at the Intercontinental. Of course, I had other postings, progressively more senior. Until a few weeks ago, I was the Director General, Africa in the Canadian foreign affairs ministry, Global Affairs Canada. I have recently moved into the Prime Minister's Office as security advisor."

"Interesting career choices for all three of us."

"Indeed – a little divergent, you might say."

We stayed chatting on that balcony until late in the evening. When we left, the brothel inside was still jumping. No doubt, it ran all night. Sabi dropped me back at the Continental.

Chapter 6.

Nadeem – February

As soon as I got back to Ottawa, I texted Matt asking to get together as soon as possible to discuss James' situation. The next day he dropped by my place in the evening.

"Let's have a SITREP, Nadeem."

"Okay. I met with Sabi Issa, James' number two man. Sabi seems solid and is Doadjan. He did mercenary time with James and the two are tight. He is also a shareholder in James' arms dealing operation, JaMAC. It is clear that he has considered all options for getting James out, and if anyone could do it, he could."

"I had no idea how big James' operation is. They have a warehouse that is bigger than any armoury in Canada, and it is stocked with modern weapons, everything – anti-tank, small arms, heavy machine guns, and more. It looks to be all Eastern Bloc stuff."

"The other thing that was clear is that James and Sabi have made multi-millions for themselves and for the President of Doadja."

"I also met with the President's Chief of Staff and then with President Obissey himself. Both meetings were a waste of time. The Chief of Staff is really a messenger boy with no decision-making capability, and the President is a typical despot that has been in power for a while. A megalomaniac. Think of Idi Amin as a model. The whole country is simply there to serve Obissey, in his mind. Even the structure of the government is set that way. There don't appear to be any ministers, any departments. Obissey runs everything out of the palace. In a normal country with functioning government activities that wouldn't be possible, but Doadja has none of that. Obissey takes all the government revenue and provides nothing to the people of the country."

"I had no success in my meeting with Obissey. He simply ended up yelling at me."

"I also had time to take a good look around the city. James is being held in harsh conditions in the old slave prison, and his time there is indeterminate. Precedent suggests that he is likely to never be released and will die there."

"As you might expect, Nambi, the capital city, is a dump. The climate doesn't help. Doadja is in that wet equatorial zone, so black mold covers many of the buildings. Neither Obissey nor his father have spent any money on the city. There is poverty and corruption everywhere. I met some decent people, but it's hard to get much done there without bribery."

"Despite the plight of the people, there is a lot of money in the country. There are a bunch of oil industry guys who spend crazy amounts in bars and clubs, but there isn't any trickle down to alleviate the general poverty level."

"In any case, the root of James' problem is a commercial disagreement between him and the President, who is a shareholder in James' company JaMAC. The President claims that James has not been paying him the fifty percent of net income that his shareholding agreement requires."

"Is there any truth in that, Nadeem?"

"Not sure. It looks like there may be other businesses that James is involved in. It seems that the President sees all of James' businesses as part of the same deal. I don't think that is what his shareholding in JaMAC would mean if businesses other than the arms trade are undertaken under different corporate identities."

"Hmm, I can see the potential for a difference in viewpoints."

"It is even worse than that. The President made it clear that he created the conditions for James to be based in Doadja and become rich, and he expects his share of everything. It looks like that's the way he runs the whole country, including the oil and minerals businesses that have provided billions of revenues to him personally. Regardless of who is right, surely a disagreement over money cannot be the basis of a life sentence or the death penalty. But in Doadja, you never know."

"I scoped out the possibility of bribery with Sabi: bribery of government officials, or bribery of prison guards, and that looks like it is impossible. Obissey is ruthless and James may be the only white guy in the prison, so it would become known quickly that he was no longer there. Fear is everywhere in that country. Obissey acts through the Presidential Guard, which everyone hates, except the protected elites."

"As for bribing the big guy, Obissey is ridiculously wealthy. There is no definitive picture, because he has accounts in many tax havens, but Forbes came up with an estimate of seven billion."

"It's hard to bribe someone who already has seven billion."

"Any other options, Nadeem?"

"A prison breakout comes to mind. The prison is more than two hundred years old. It is the old slave transhipment point. Traders brought Slaves from inland in Doadja and many of the neighbouring countries, then they were assembled there to be shipped to the Caribbean or America. It is a huge stone fort on an island close to the coast and right in the city. There may be some way of getting James out of there and out of the country. Of course, he could never return, and his business would be toast."

"Nadeem, why hasn't Obissey shut James' firm down and seized everything? He has the power to have done that," Matt asked.

"I raised that with Sabi. He is concerned and has disbursed the equipment and weapons that they have in storage in Doadja. But he thinks that because JaMAC continues to send cash to Obissey's accounts and because it would be very hard for him to sell off JaMAC's assets, he won't move against the company. Perhaps Obissey is also thinking he might release James at some point."

"If we were going to consider the breakout option, Nadeem, what would the next steps be?"

"We would need to bring in a team that could undertake the breakout. They would need to develop the plan, case the prison, etc. It's beyond a couple of old farts like us."

"Do you have someone in mind?"

"Don't freak out, Matt, but I am thinking of Dan."

"My Dan?"

"Exactly, Matt; more than anyone, your son has the skills and experience to pull this off."

"Not alone."

"No, he would need to bring in people he knows and trusts to work with him."

"I am not convinced; putting my own son into danger makes me a bit queasy. But I will raise it with him. Problem is, he will jump at the adventure of it. Let me get back to you after I talk to him."

It may seem funny that I proposed one of our kids to get involved in this potentially hazardous venture, but let me tell you about Dan.

I have known Dan since he was born. I didn't see him all the time as he was growing up, but the families got together whenever it worked, so I saw him at every stage of growth. Now he is thirty-seven and looks a lot like his dad at that age – fit, tall, brown hair and beard. Looks like a wilderness lodge operator.

Dan is currently a Lieutenant Colonel with JTF2, Canada's special forces unit. He is one of those combat junkies, living the dream. After graduating from RMC in 2006, he was posted to 2 PPCLI in Edmonton, but then almost immediately was sent to Ukraine on a training mission. Pretty quickly, he was identified as a special forces candidate and by 2011 he was in Afghanistan for two years as a Captain in JTF2, where his cool, intuitive leadership and his commitment to his troops led to rapid additional promotions.

The government established JTF2 in the 1990s, but it really took shape after 2001. It is a rapid reaction force. In Afghanistan, JTF soldiers were in-country by December 2001 as part of the American-led special forces team in Task Force K-Bar, which was tasked with seeking out Al Qaeda and Taliban fighters in the mountains around Tora Bora. From 2005 through 2017, JTF members were in Iraq, training, but also fighting ISIS units. Like Delta or the Brit Special Air Service, JTF2 selects the best, trains them hard, and is deployed frequently, often without public knowledge.

Otherwise, Dan is just a normal guy. He is married to Naomi, a lawyer in Ottawa, and they have a two-year-old daughter, Alicia.

Two days later, Matt called me.

"Dan is intrigued and would like to know more."

"Great, Matt, let's get together, does tomorrow evening work? How much did you tell him?"

"I hope I gave him the same picture that you and I have, but you may want to check that with him when we get together. Let me check to see if tomorrow night works for him."

It did, and we once again got together at my place.

"Dan, good to see you. Your dad keeps me up to date on your comings and goings. I know he is happy to have you in Canada for now."

"Thanks, Nadeem, although I am scheduled for a rotation in Poland to train Ukrainian forces in September. I will be away for three months then."

"I understand that Matt brought you up to speed on the James Mackenzie issue."

"He did. I understand your loyalty to the guy, but a prison break is a big illegal issue, even in a shithole like Doadja. Also, based on my quick check on the country, fatally dangerous if it fails."

"True, and we would rely on your assessment of the possibility and risks. We know that James has always taken risks, and being in the arms trade in Africa is certainly right up there on the crazy scale. Nevertheless, it looks like he is facing death over a disagreement about money, so we will do whatever we can to help him. I hope that makes sense to you."

"Sure, I know how close we all become to our classmates and army buds, I get that part. But what is the idea now?"

"Dan, if you have leave time available, and interest, would you consider going to Doadja to assess the feasibility of a breakout, assisted by bribery if necessary? If it looks possible, then we would want you to come back with a proposed plan that we could kick around."

"Hmm, you know me. I'm always up for a bit of adventure. I can't go next week, but I think the week after that works. What is my excuse, Nadeem, if I'm questioned at Doadjan border services?"

"That shouldn't be a problem since James is in the weapons trade and you are a specialist in the field. James' local manager and number two is Sabi Issa. We will let Sabi know that you are coming and he will meet you at the airport. Don't mention anything yet about a possible breakout, just tell him you are doing a follow-up assessment. Sabi is an ex-mercenary who served under James in Angola and Sierra Leone, so he will respect your expertise. He may also start to suspect that we are going a bit beyond diplomacy, but no need to confirm that right now."

Chapter 7.

James – March

The feeble light coming through the small, high window in the cell tells me that another day has begun. How many days, I have no idea. I tried to keep track for a while, but without some way of keeping a record, I lost it.

Every day is the same as every other day. Sometimes, early in the morning a guard pushes a bowl of water through the slot in the door. I try to keep active. The cell is about three and a half metres by two and a half. I figure, knocking off about a half a metre for how close I can walk to the wall, I have a perimeter of three by two to walk; a ten-metre loop, so one hundred times around is a kilometre. When I first got here, once I recovered from that initial beating, I tried to do five klicks every day, but I can't do that any longer. One is a challenge. I just keep losing weight and energy. Other than that initial bowl of water, the weak soup or stew at the end of the day is the only other food or drink. Clearly this isn't survivable over the long-term.

Man, if only there was some way of getting word out to my old buds Nadeem and Matt; they would figure out how to help. Nadeem has diplomatic connections and could maybe bring some nation-to-nation pressure on Obissey to let me go. Matt is deep into signals intel; he could dig up some secrets that would get the Americans to pressure Doadja. I'm sure that both of these guys would definitely pitch in if they knew about my situation.

After military college, I saw less of Nadeem because he went into the air force, but Matt and I served together in the infantry, including in some unusual places. We were together in Edmonton in the PPCLI for the first couple of years. When I was posted to the UN in Namibia in '89, Matt headed off on a different posting. My tour in Namibia was uneventful in any case. UNTAG was simply acting as a peacekeeper while the South Africans withdrew and elections were held. It was a rag tag group of peacekeepers, observers, police, and some civilian advisors working to support the transition to a Namibian government. It wrapped up in '90.

There wasn't any real action in Namibia, but I had time to poke around there. I also spent some time in Botswana on leave and really fell for Africa. I started to pay attention to the politics and dynamics of the continent. A couple of things jumped out: there were a lot of opportunities to make serious money there, and there were always uprisings, revolutions, or coups going on in one or more countries. If a person loved adventure and was an experienced military officer, there could be some real excitement there.

I was back in Canada for only a year when our regiment was posted to Croatia. Nadeem, Matt, and I continued our friendship in that challenging environment. It wasn't an ideal situation for UN peacekeeping. None of the participants wanted peace, they wanted to win, so the UN kept finding itself squeezed between Croats and Serbs going at each other. We were frequently under heavy shelling from one side or the other, or in firefights to keep from getting overrun by one of the warring parties. Some UN actions were simply cowardly, such as abandoning villages we knew would be destroyed, rather than drawing a hard line. A big part of the problem with the UN work was the dysfunctional chain of command. Trying to work up a multi-national chain all the way to UN HQ in New York, simply to return fire, was a recipe for disaster. Matt really saved my company's ass at one of these cluster-fucks. We were taking all kinds of fire from the Croat lines – artillery, small arms – and my units were starting to take casualties. I was on the radio on and off for hours trying to get permission to return fire. We couldn't withdraw, because we were squeezed in a valley with the Croats in front of us and the Serbs behind us. Obviously, the Croats would claim that they were shelling the Serbs and we were just collateral damage, but it was clear to us on the ground that they were trying to get us to withdraw. They had superior numbers and firepower to the Serbs and just wanted to get at them.

I was getting nowhere with UNPROFOR HQ until I managed to get Matt on the radio. He had been assigned to a G4 position in HQ. I remember telling him:

"Jeez, Matt, we are getting killed here, I mean literally. We have been taking casualties for four or five hours. I have made it clear to HQ that we cannot withdraw, because we are pinched into this valley. I need to suppress the Croatian fire, but I am getting nothing from the gang in HQ."

"James, take this as approval to return fire. I will take the rap if the UN sees this as a problem. We can't wait for a big discussion in New York. Go at them and leave it to me."

So we did, and as expected, it worked. We started to put disciplined, targeted fire into the Croat lines, and within about half an hour, they had stopped firing on us. I heard later that there was blowback from New York that we had moved without approval, but Matt stood up and blew them off. As Operations Officer on the ground, he took action to save UN lives, end of story.

That's what I loved about my friends from college. Not just Matt, but all of them. Not afraid to take responsibility, to do what is right and to protect their own. Great guys. I need to get them involved here, in Doadja; I need for them to know what has happened to me. Does Sabi even know where I am? If he does, he may twig that getting some of my Canadian buds involved may help with my situation.

If Sabi, Nadeem, or Matt can get me out of here, I am so out of Doadja. I sure as hell don't need to work. I have more than one hundred million dollars waiting for me out there. I have great spots that I own or rent around the world and my own jet to get me in between them.

Because business often took me there, I have a sweet apartment in Amsterdam. Not large, like most places in that city, but nonetheless great. A third floor in an old house on

Herengracht, walking distance to everything. Old wood floors, white walls, lovely.

The condo in Toronto is another story. Ultra modern, it is mostly windows. On Hazelton, it is again right in the centre of Yorkville, so I can walk anywhere. It is large and if I need to use it for a while, I can arrange to have a cook.

The real gem, though, is the Mustique House. I bought it ten years ago. Part of what I love about Mustique is that it isn't easy to get to, and random tourists aren't welcome. There is only one small hotel on the island, the Cotton House, so other than homeowners and renters of homes, there is only accommodation for about fifty tourists on the island. The guests in the hotels are usually overflow friends of homeowners. My house has its own staff and I have rented it out from time to time, but the high cost means that the pool of potential renters is small. In addition to the rent, there are other significant costs that renters must pay. The cook finds out what they want to eat, then flies to St. Vincent to get the food. The food prices and the costs for the flights are, of course, the renter's problem.

Most of the Mustique houses, including mine, are open compounds because the weather there is great. Each bedroom is a standalone module, linked by open corridors to a centre module that contains the common use areas: living room, entertainment room, dining room, kitchen, and staff quarters.

My house is on a ridge looking down to the beach on the west side. The beaches are simply perfect. Whenever I'm there I go down to Macaroni Beach, with its perfect sand, and the beach is usually empty, or will have three or four other people on it, and the women will be topless.

The other fun thing about Mustique is the people. Mostly upper-crust Brits, with some interesting characters mixed in; an Iranian millionaire, and a Brit who made his money in porn, are typical. Lots of laughs down at Basil's bar on the beach. Cool events, too. Mr. Porn had a crew working at his house for more than two months setting up his New Year's fireworks display. It's awesome to see someone blow off over a million dollars in fireworks at their own home.

Of course, some interesting women show up on Mustique as well. The thing about millionaires is that they are often surrounded by younger, attractive women.

Shit, back to reality, here! I am fading quickly in this tiny cell in a crap country in Africa. There's quite a gap between reality today and where I want to be. Get me out of here, guys! Please!

Chapter 8.
Dan - March

Immigration on arrival in Doadja was a non-event other than the ridiculous queue. I just said "business" as my purpose and the agent waved me through. A guy who I assumed was Sabi was waiting outside the bag hall holding a sign with "Dan Hawney" on it.

"Sabi?'

"Sure, welcome to Doadja, Dan."

On the way to the hotel – unfortunately the same dreaded Continental that Nadeem had told me about – I briefed Sabi.

"Sabi, I am just following up on loose ends from Nadeem's visit. I don't need any meetings with the high-priced help. From what Nadeem told me, those were pointless, so I will just make my own way around for the next couple of days. It would be great if you could set me up with a car and driver."

"Of course, I'll get you Samson, the same one that Nadeem had. Tomorrow at nine?"

"Eight would be better, I am only here for tomorrow and the day after. Before I head back, I will come by the office and tell you if I've made any progress."

"Okay. By the way, how do you know James? You are much younger."

"He's my dad's friend. My interest is in helping my dad Matt, and Nadeem."

"Ah, that makes sense, Nadeem told me about Matt, and he mentioned you. What do you bring to the table to help?"

"Just a unique perspective from a different generation. I hope I might come up with some new ideas. I will fill you in more tonight."

"Okay, here we are, at the famous Continental. I hope Nadeem did not fill you in too much about the merits of this hotel."

"More than enough, Sabi."

We both had a bit of a laugh. Sabi proposed,

"How about dinner tonight – local food, local music?"

"Sure, that would be great."

"I will pick you up at seven."

"Excellent, see you then, and thanks."

As promised, Sabi picked me up and took me to a roadside establishment. Beer, chicken, and a local band. All surprisingly good.

"Sabi, I have heard a lot about you from Nadeem."

"Mostly good, I hope?"

"Well, on a world scale, good might not be the right word for an ex-mercenary arms dealer, but if the test is loyalty to James, and ability to take action, then good enough."

That elicited a smile from Sabi.

"James and I like to think we are different from the Russian guys. We have never dealt with terrorist groups. Mostly, we deal with governments, or potential governments wanting to take power, or mining companies that need serious protection. Even some major Western intelligence agencies have been clients of ours from time to time; situations where we have provided them with a deniable cut out when providing arms to their favoured groups."

"Dan, I know very little about you. Nadeem mentioned that he had a daughter and that you are Matt's son, but that's really all I know."

"Both Alida, Nadeem's daughter, and I followed in our parents' footsteps and went to the military college in Canada."

"It must be a big place; everybody seems to have gone there."

"No, no, just the opposite. The graduating class each year is only about two hundred for the army, air force, and navy combined. There is a bit of a tradition of families going there, however. A few families have had members there since the college opened in 1876."

"You were army?"

"Still am. Special forces."

"And Alida?"

"No longer serving. She did a tour in Afghanistan but has since left and works for a major accounting firm."

By this time, we had finished eating, but ordered more beers and listened to the music. We were well away from other tables, so I wasn't worried about someone overhearing us.

"Sabi, fill me in a bit more about the whole security environment here. Honestly, Doadja isn't on anyone's radar, other than its terrible reputation for the president's family looting the state."

"It's simple, Dan. The nation loathes the president, so he trusts only selected members from his own tribal group. He has loaded these into a unit called the Presidential Guard that essentially provides the state security functions. It is not large, two hundred members, but they terrorize the population by disappearing anyone that might challenge the government, even in the smallest way. They are based mostly here in the city, with smaller detachments in each of the villages to act as the eyes and ears of President Obissey."

"The military here is a different story. It is drawn from a base of draftees from all tribal groups. It isn't a factor in domestic security. It is mostly army, with three battalions – one here, and the two others elsewhere in the country. The army base here is co-located with the prison, on the island where they are holding James."

"Does the army run the prison?"

"No, it's just that the old slave prison was so huge and permanent that it provides sufficient space for a prison on the ocean side, and for the base on the side facing the city. Access to the prison is through the base, but the army doesn't run the prison."

"There is also a small air force with a couple of old Russian jet aircraft, mostly there as a threat to our own population. None of the neighbouring countries are a threat. There is a small navy, with a couple of coastal patrol vessels that should be doing fisheries patrols, but don't seem to be very effective."

"The police here are just traffic cops, since there isn't any criminal law other than directions from Obissey, and those are actioned through the Guard. The cops are totally corrupt. You may gain some first-hand experience with them tomorrow. If they see a white guy in the car, they will pull you over. It is simply a shakedown. Your driver Samson will know how to deal with them. Just look dumbfounded and let him pay them off. He will add it to the bill."

"The only other organized semi-security group is Customs/Immigration. They monitor the borders and their focus is on duties, tariffs, and unwelcome visitors. Again, very corrupt. We deal with them all the time with goods coming and going, and they will do anything we want if we make a suitable payment."

"That's the security picture. Not pretty, but it is part of the reason James is based here. Everything is flexible."

"Okay, understood. You should drop me back at the hotel, please. I want to be sharp for my look around tomorrow."

"Okay, let's go."

. . . .

The next morning, I had Samson drop me at the waterfront.

"I am just going to sit here, read my book, and get over my jet lag," I told him. "Is there fishing here?"

"Of course, there are local fishermen. Not fishing for pleasure, but for their living."

"Would any of them be willing to take me out this afternoon?"

"Listen, these are very poor people, for a little money they will take you to North America in their little boat."

"Can you find one, please, and set me up to go out at, say, one?"

"Yes, sir."

"Okay, come back before one and take me to the boat."

"Yes, sir."

I wasn't trying to deal with jet lag, but rather, I was looking to find a good vantage point where I could clearly see the prison, including the entrance from the land side. I found a perfect spot at the base of an old pier, where I could see what I needed to see, but was hidden from general view, without looking too suspicious. I put my water bottle down and opened the book on my lap, looking touristy, I hoped (although I don't know if there has been anyone crazy enough to come to Doadja for tourism).

The prison was as described in Wikipedia and by Nadeem. An enormous stone edifice, completely filling the island, not more than three hundred metres offshore from the city. A narrow, two-lane vehicle bridge, without sidewalks, led from the mainland entranceway to the prison. It was clear that there was a large courtyard on the other side of the prison entrance, because I could see sunlight shining out from the inside, and because there were army vehicles entering and leaving from time to time.

Sabi had told me that the army occupied half or more of the old prison, taking up the whole side facing town. The prisoners were held in the remaining portion that primarily faced the open sea. That's why I needed to go fishing.

Because the old prison occupied the whole island, the stone walls almost came down to the water level. Two to three meters of sheer rock were at the base of the walls. The walls were made of large stone blocks and appeared to be dry joined, or with a minimum of mortar. They would be climbable by someone experienced, with the right gear. The windows along the side were tiny, with a grid of iron bars that looked like they were part of the original build – they weren't attached on the outside but built into the walls and were severely rusted. A row of modern flood lights protruded from the parapet at the top of the walls, clearly intended to light the walls at night. The windows were also high on the walls. The lower floors must be used for storage or for some other purpose.

There would be some major challenges in executing a successful breakout:

- Where in this huge building was James' cell? We would need detailed inside knowledge of the layout, so we could pinpoint the location from the outside. Effective bribery would be critical.

- The embedded bars and the adjacent army base created a problem. The bars could not be pulled out unless they were so rusted that they came away, but they could easily be cut with C4 or a thermal lance, though either one of those approaches would certainly draw immediate attention.

- Even if somehow, we could identify the precise cell, and silently get the bars out in the dark without the guards noticing in the floodlight glow, we would still be high up the wall. This would make the extraction of a weakened prisoner through the opening quite difficult.

- Getting in through the front door would seem to be close to impossible. After crossing the bridge, the extraction team would effectively be in the army base. It would have to pass through the base unseen, find the entrance to the prison, break in, and make their way to the right cell, extract James, then return undetected through the base. Yikes.

Maybe the fishing trip would reveal some weak spot, although the challenge of finding the right cell would still be there, unless we broke everybody out at the same time.

The afternoon in the sun, out on the boat was no more revealing. The fisherman spoke no English and little French. I just pointed him to places where I wanted to go. Obviously, I didn't want to go only around the ocean side of the prison, so we putzed around for a few hours here and there, including the prison area.

It was no more promising. Clearly, during the slave trading days the prison had had a wharf on the ocean side, and there were the marks of an old exit to this wharf on the lower wall, but it had been filled with the stone blocks years ago. Only a colour difference in the aged stone showed where it had been.

Samson dropped me back at the Continental late in the afternoon. Around sundown, I stopped at the desk and asked them to get me a cab. Luckily, the cabbie's French was as good as mine.

"*Je veux trouver un restaurant local, un endroit avec la cuisine to Doadja et plus tard la musique locale.*"

"*Bien sur, monsieur.*"

He took me into an area of dense housing, with narrow streets. We came to a construction barricade.

"*Le restaurant est juste là-bas, mais la route est fermée.*"

"*Très bien, je peux marcher là.*"

"*Non, non monsieur, vous ne pouvez marcher ici, c'est dangereux pour un visiteur comme vous ici. Je prendrais une autre route de l'autre côté.*"

So, around a few blocks of these narrow streets we went, until we pulled up in front of the same restaurant that I had seen from two hundred metres away at the other end of the street.

"*J'attendrai ici, monsieur.*"

"*Très bien et merci, mais ce sera longtemps, je pense.*"

"*Pas de problème, monsieur.*"

Clearly the cabbie would get a substantial tip when I got back to the hotel. My real purpose in going local, without Sabi or even Samson, was to get a feel for the place. What were the people like, what was going on locally? Sitting for dinner and some music would allow me to get a bit of a sense of what was happening.

Inside the place was basic, with a bar, about ten tables, an area set up for a band, and a small dance floor. Although it was too early for the band to be in action, it was already busy, with a crowd of locals at the bar, and most of the tables occupied.

It looked like the only drink of choice was local beer, so I took a stool at the bar, ordered a beer in French, and asked what food was available. There was no menu, and the choice for dinner was goat stew or goat stew.

The beer was cold lager, and the stew was surprisingly good. Like goat stew everywhere, it was chewy, but it had a nice peppery edge.

I simply sat with my beer and stew, looked around and tried to understand a bit more about Doadja. Of course, I couldn't understand a word of what the locals were saying, but it was interesting just to read the vibe. Although the people in the restaurant were enjoying an evening out, I could see that they were seriously poor. Old, recycled T-shirts from North America were the clothing of choice – Baltimore Orioles, Harley-Davidson, Bar Harbor Lobster Pound, among others.

Until the band showed up, the place was subdued. People spoke quietly with their nearby companions, as though wanting to avoid anyone from another table overhearing the conversation. There was an edge of fear in it, I thought.

The only noticeable movement was with the two prostitutes that circulated around the room, seeking action. As the only obvious foreigner and therefore likely the richest person in the place, one of the two of course approached me.

"Bonsoir, monsieur."

"Sorry, I don't speak French," I said, hoping that would shut down the conversation.

"Oh, English, I love English. You are American, big oil person?"

I thought that I may as well leave her with the impression I was American.

"American, you like maybe buy me a nice drink, maybe take me somewhere for good fuck?"

"No, I am not interested, and you can tell your friend that I am not interested in her, either. I am just here to eat and listen to a little music."

She pouted but turned and walked away.

The music itself was the best part of the evening. It was a unique sound. Overlaid on local roots, were French/Spanish colonial influences, combined with residues of music that must have been left over from the times when Cuban mercenaries were backing Obissey's father. The saxophone, guitar, bass, and drums of the band moved seamlessly between different beats, and even different languages. The common feature was a heavy, intoxicating beat that got the dancers going.

When I settled up, the prices clearly were the attractive element of the bar. Beer was thirty cents, and the goat stew was the equivalent of about two dollars. Comparing this to what Nadeem had told us about the waterfront restaurants for the elite, neatly summarized the extremes of Doadja.

As promised, the taxi was waiting to take me back to the hotel. My tip was generous.

I had only been back a few minutes when there was a knock on my door. When I opened it, a beautiful young woman walked right in, acting like we were old buds. She was stunning: African, probably Doadjan, but possibly from anyplace in northern Africa. Very tall, mocha coloured, with a charming smile. I immediately thought back to reading Sir Richard Burton's exploration books where he described the pleasures of sleeping with women from this region as his best bedroom experiences.

"Excuse me, Miss, you must have the wrong room. This is my room."

"Oh no, not wrong. Sabi sent me."

"Sabi sent you. Why?"

"He said you might be lonely here in Doadja and could need a woman to help you sleep."

It was a kind offer. In my younger life, before I was happily married, I might have considered it, but this was not the time or place. Also, I didn't need to be worried about STDs, and I didn't need to be in anyone's debt.

"Well, tell Sabi I appreciate the gesture, but no, thank you, I don't need any help getting to sleep. Please leave."

"Okay, but you need to tell Sabi tomorrow that it was a good thing, that I was beautiful but it was your problem. He is going to be blaming me."

"You are beautiful, it was a kind offer, and it is my problem. Good night."

The following day, I had Samson take me on the same "see the city" excursion as he had done with Nadeem – the palace, the Presidential Guard base on the edge of town, the government comm centre, and the airport.

I had Nadeem's description of the palace, but I wanted to see as much of it for myself as I could. We stopped briefly at the courtyard, the side facing west. The gate was guarded by even more of the Presidential Guard than he had mentioned. There were ten of them milling about.

Without making it too obvious what I was doing, I directed Samson to drive along the side of the palace and then turn onto the street at the back. I could see that the palace wall was also the outside building wall on both the side and at the back. Any outdoor space inside the walls was limited to the courtyard, and maybe another inner courtyard.

Next, Samson took me out of town on the road to the Presidential Guard base. It was only a few clicks from the edge of town, but along the way there was at least a kilometre that wasn't built up. Just scrubby fields with blowing plastic bags. The Guard base looked like it was an old colonial era base. It was mostly two-storey barracks.

Then I asked him to take me to Sabi's office. Once I got there, I said,

"Sabi, I have had a chance to look around. Oh, and by the way, I turned down my night visitor last night. Quite beautiful, but I was not interested."

"No worries."

"I would like to tell you a bit more about why I am here, but I suggest we go for a walk together to discuss that."

"A walk?"

Clearly Sabi thought I was nuts; it was at least thirty-two degrees out and humid. I gestured toward the ceiling and walls, then cupped my hands behind my ears. He got the message and we headed outside.

"We sweep the office frequently, Dan, if you are worried about bugs."

"I just feel more secure out here."

"Okay, Sabi, you've been wondering why I am here. After his visit, Nadeem concluded that diplomacy and bribery wouldn't likely get James free, so I'm looking for more dynamic alternatives, like a prison break. Why me? Because my expertise is kinetic actions."

"Hmm, I wondered. That makes sense now. What did you figure out?"

"Sabi, you live here, you were a mercenary with James, you probably know what I concluded. A prison break just isn't a realistic option."

"You do know, Dan, that I could bring a lot of additional resources to bear. Because of our business, James and I have maintained our old mercenary networks. I could bring a lot of people into play. We also have the resources to pay them."

"I sensed that, but I don't think that a gang of people, even skilled people, would necessarily increase the chance of a successful prison break, unless we essentially stormed the prison and tried to break everyone out."

"Probably right."

"But Sabi, tell me more about your networks."

"Dan, I think you know that James was a mercenary here in Africa for a few years."

"That was rumoured."

"Well, I won't drag you through the history, but we built an elite team, active in several countries, from Angola to Sierra Leone. When James stopped, he brought me here with him, but many of the others on our team have remained active. There is never a shortage of spots for sharp soldiers."

"How do you keep in touch with them, Sabi?"

"Our business requires secure networks and it also keeps us in touch with them because they refer client groups to us. For example, if they are working for a group in, say, Congo, which is looking for heavy weapons, they tell their bosses about JaMAC. We get them the goods and deliver them on-site. Our old networks only send us potential clients that they know can and will pay, so the network is valuable."

"Sabi, is any of your old group on UN or South Africa shit-lists?"

"The Government of South Africa found a couple of their own people guilty of mercenary action. They are out of jail but are obviously known and under watch. We don't contact them. They aren't part of the network anymore."

"Okay, thanks, Sabi, I will keep that in mind when we explore options. I am going to head home on tomorrow's flight."

On the flight back, I started to think about an alternative plan and the additional resources we might need.

Sabi could help set up any in-country resources. From the Canadian end, I would like to bring in a couple of classmates from RMC – Maxime Lapeyre and Alida.

Maxime is in JTF2 with me. He is a soldier's soldier, his nickname is Absolute Max, Abs for short. A skilled operator, he is also a little gonzo, living the dream as a warrior. He would be incredible if things go kinetic. From Trois Rivières, Max has always pushed everything to the limit. He grew up completely engrossed in mechanical toys – go-karts, Ski-Doos, and the like. The only thing that would keep him from these toys was hockey.

Several people have commented when we have been together in bars that he reminds them of the character Hagrid from the *Harry Potter* movies. He is a little oversized, with muscle not fat, and has a serious beard.

At RMC, he selected armour as his profession and went armour after grad. That's what led him to Afghanistan. Canada was the only NATO army to move tanks into the theatre, and the Leopard C2's became a valuable tool for any of the serious actions. The Taliban so feared the tanks that their appearance on the scene would change the flow of the action, even before they engaged. Max operated in Kandahar, Panjwai, and Zhari districts in some of the most fierce, large battles of the whole Afghanistan effort.

Because of his high performance and his interest in active operations, after returning from Afghanistan, Max applied to join the special forces. I think some of his superiors in the armoured corps may have been glad to see him move on – he doesn't suffer fools. That's how we came to be serving together.

Super fit, and of course completely bilingual (capable of colourful swearing in at least two languages), he has been a valuable player in any action. He is a bit physically scarred-up from shrapnel wounds he suffered in Afghanistan and a bit mentally scarred from several years of combat, but that hasn't slowed him a bit. He still displays the same sense of humor that he had when he was twenty.

Alida would bring entirely different skills. First, she would blend in better than the rest of us. She is the daughter of Nawaz and Anitha, his Rwandan wife.

I think she is amazing-looking, but I am definitely prejudiced. We had "a thing" for the last year at college, but then we headed off in different directions. Although we tried to see each other when we could, it was too infrequent and we just drifted apart. No regrets, no bad feelings. We are still good friends.

Alida will bring the business smarts if we need to deal with money issues. After graduating at the top of her year at RMC, she later went on to get an MBA from Queens. She was always self-confident, but in the business area, she is excellent. Her running joke is, "I like to screw up once and a while, to make me equal to men." She really knows her stuff. Her French is good, making her bilingual, and she has a good grasp of Spanish as well.

Truly international, not just from her heritage, Alida grew up moving around whenever her dad was posted to another assignment. A lot of her grade school time was spent in Barbados, and she did her high school in Ottawa.

After graduation from RMC, Alida served six years in the artillery as a battery commander, including a tour in Afghanistan.

Since then, she has been with the international consulting firm, KPMG. In the last few years, she has been part of forensic audit teams. She is married, but without kids so far.

Between her military experience and consulting, she is street-smart. She sees through BS quickly.

If we develop a plan that involves a bunch of players, we are going to need access to a lot of money and the ability to get it to where it needs to be. Sabi may know where JaMAC's money is, but James may have kept the details to himself. Alida will be able to help us access those funds.

Chapter 9.

Dan - March

To: MHawney@gac.gc.ca; nnawaz@cse-cst.gc.ca

From: Dan Hawney (Miso@gmail.com)

Subject: Africa Vacation

Can we meet at my dad's place Thursday evening, say 19:00, to talk about my recent trip to Doadja?

Let me know as soon as you can.

Dan

Thursday worked, and the three of us got together at Matt's.

"Dan, what did you find out?"

"Nadeem, you saw the prison. I don't think a prison break is viable at all. We don't know his location, the prison is huge, and getting in through any kind of trickery is unlikely. There is a pervasive atmosphere of fear in the country. Although bribery is common, bribing someone to act against Obissey's interest is not, and could backfire on us."

"Is that it, no possible solution?" asked Nadeem.

"Well, I have an idea, I said. Let me take a few minutes to explain. I have a sketch map here that will help you understand what I am talking about."

I unfolded a sheet of paper with a hand-sketch of Nambi and the surrounding area on it.

"Let me orient everyone. Nambi is on the west coast of the country. The key features are the prison, on an island just offshore, the palace, which is central, the airport about five klicks south of the place, the government communications centre two klicks southeast of the palace, the Presidential Guard barracks which is out of town five klicks northeast, and the JaMAC warehouses southeast of the government communications centre. I have marked these all on the map."

"I took some time to look around and get a sense of the place. Obissey is extremely unpopular, ruling by terror, with the Presidential Guard as his gestapo. The Guard has about twenty-five personnel on duty at any one time protecting the President. There are another one hundred and twenty-five off-duty, but they are in a residential community about five kilometres east of the palace. The roads between the city centre area and that area are frequently very congested."

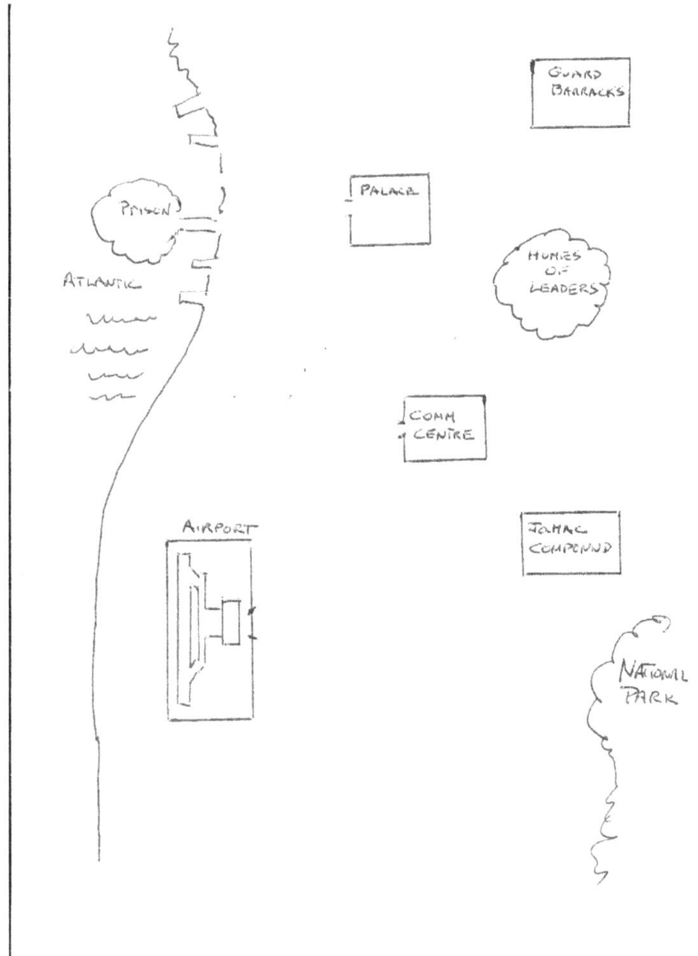

"The army, on the other hand, is poorly trained, made up primarily of draftees, many of whom are from a different tribe than Obissey."

"The army within the city is composed of about six hundred soldiers of One Brigade. There are two other brigades, but they are well out of the city in other areas of the country."

"One Brigade is entirely barracked in the eastern portion of the old slave prison on Wailing Island. They are quite close to the palace and the city core area, but access is across a short bridge from the island to the mainland."

"One large building near the city core contains all the national communication services – TV, radio, ISP, telephone. This building is secure and fenced, but lightly protected with normally four to six Presidential Guards on duty."

"Similarly, the airport is lightly protected. The tower has keypad access, but no guards on duty. There are two older fighter aircraft in an adjacent hangar, with two guards on duty."

"The police are simply traffic cops, and even in that role, quite amenable to bribes. The border services are hopeless and can be easily bribed to let vehicles and people through, especially if they are known. Sabi is used to bribing them to allow his truck traffic to come and go without any issues."

"I am getting a bad feeling here, Dan, I sense a message in all of this background," commented Matt."

"Indeed, there is a message. Obissey and his father have ruled so long without any serious challenges that everything has a sleepy, ready to change feel. There is almost universal unhappiness, the public knows that the big guy is pillaging the country and leaving scraps for everyone else. The only loyal group is the Presidential Guard and maybe a few of the high-priced help around the President. It is a small group. I think we could force a regime change, and free James with a small team. I believe that Sabi has the network to potentially assemble such a group."

"Wow Dan, you don't think small!" exclaimed Matt. "You must understand that the risks in this are huge. Failure could mean horrible death for those involved."

"Even success could damage us here if any involvement on our part came out," Nadeem said, "it would cost us our jobs and even potentially prison time."

"Of course." I said, "(A), it would have to succeed, and (B), any involvement of Canadians would have to be secret, not just before or during such a coup, but forever."

"What are you thinking about how this would work, just in general terms?" asked Nadeem.

I went on to explain,

"It is general at this point. We would need to develop a detailed plan. But, in general, we would first locate a potential new Doadja leader, hopefully an improvement on the incumbent. Sabi would line up force resources and weapons. The coup itself would be a flash coup – twenty to forty minutes from first action to end of fighting. It would involve the following steps: taking out Obissey at the palace, isolating the army on the island, preventing the Presidential Guard off-duty elements from accessing the palace area, controlling the airport tower, disabling the two jets, and seizing the comms centre, and finally, having the new leader take control. All of this would happen almost simultaneously."

"Oh, is that all? I can see how that could be easy!" Matt interjected sarcastically.

"With careful planning and the right team, I believe it could have a high chance of success," I concluded.

"What resources are you thinking of?"

"We need to develop the details, but from here, I only see the three of us and a couple of classmates that I would like to bring in – Max Lapeyre and Alida."

"Alida?" Nadeem jumped in: "You want to bring my daughter in?"

"Yes, we will likely need her financial skills. We are not proposing to have her directly involved in any kinetic action. Indeed, you and Matt would also not be on-site for the coup, and your involvement would be invisible."

"In terms of arms and soldiers, we would need to develop the numbers and plans on how to get them into Doadja, but Sabi says he has links with well-trained and current combat resources."

"Man, I am stunned," said Matt. "What would be the next step if we go any further with this idea?"

"We would all use our contacts to locate a potential new leader for Doadja, then Nadeem would cautiously approach him or her to determine their level of interest. If done carefully, that wouldn't be too dangerous. I assume that any potential candidates are not living in Doadja, otherwise they would be in prison or murdered."

"Dan, Nadeem, and I think we should at least go as far as replacing Obissey, in any case. The world would be a better place without him.," said Matt.

After a lengthy pause, Nadeem said,

"I don't mind going to talk to a potential leader if we can identify one. I would suggest, however, that if the candidate seems as evil as Obissey we may not want to proceed. Yes, we want to get James out, but changing one bad guy for another one equally bad seems like a poor way to do it. Let's do some digging and then decide."

"Another thing, based on what I saw in Doadja, I am concerned about Internet communication security. Doadja probably has Pegasus or something similar, so we need to be careful when communicating amongst ourselves, and between here and Doadja. I told Sabi to get a licence for the computer game Civilization VI and to log on every night at 2200, that will be 1800 here. We can use the chat function inside the game. That will look harmless and won't attract attention. I am also thinking that we need to cloak our language, even within the game chats."

Chapter 10.
Nadeem - March

I used whatever contacts I could discreetly query at work to dig for information on potential political leaders for Doadja. Matt did the same using his personal networks at GCHQ and NSA. What we learned was that there were three possibilities:

- Francois Orou, who is living in Spain and leading a semi-organized group of Doadjans living outside the country. He is openly holding himself up as the future leader but appears to be mostly a blowhard. Someone is providing him a low level of funding, possibly the Spanish government, or maybe the CIA. He is seventy-two years old and has been in exile for more than forty years:

- Bernard NDong lives in the UK. He is lower profile but comes from the same minority tribe as the President. The general perception is that he would be Obissey's choice as a successor if he became terminally ill and he would likely follow the same dictatorial policies. He travels to Doadja from time to time, so clearly Obissey doesn't see him as a threat.

- Rafael Lare currently lives in Senegal. He's a university lecturer, and from a respected family from the majority tribe. He's well-educated and exceptionally low profile. He is not known to have undertaken any actions to upset Obissey. His potential popularity is grassroots.

Of the three, only Lare would meet my criteria of potentially offering a leadership more focused on the people of Doadja than on his personal wealth.

Growing up in Njuma, a smaller city in Doadja, his parents were both healthcare workers who founded one of the few functioning hospitals in Doadja. Research indicates that they were careful not to openly criticize the government. Nonetheless, they had a strong sense of social justice and understood that the Obissey family was pillaging the country. They were not politically active, because they knew it would endanger both themselves and their hospital. They were determined, however, to ensure that their son would have an education that would enable him to live and work outside of Doadja.

After lower school in Doadja, Lare moved to Saint-Louis, Senegal to attend Gaston Berger University. There, he earned a Bachelor's degree in economics and was subsequently granted a scholarship to enrol in a Master's program at the London School of Economics, where he earned his degree.

He's now thirty-seven years old. He speaks French, English, Spanish, and several African languages, including Wolof, Punar, and the official language of Doadja, Akano. In addition to teaching economics, he has a business on the side that develops small business software applications (accounting, HR management) that run on mobile phones.

Searches of various public and secure data sources indicate that although Lare has never challenged the government in Doadja, he does have an ardent desire to see a better country. An incident when he was fourteen in Njuma may have had a major influence on his desire for change. At that time, Obissey sent the Presidential Guard to the city because he perceived a threat to his authority, and hundreds of bodies were left in the street as a result. Lare's parents were lucky to have survived that sweep.

He is married to a woman from Senegal who he met at university and they have two small kids. He is highly active online, keeping in touch with a wide network of friends in Doadja, the UK, and Senegal. Although he has no clear enemies, as the son of "elites," the Government of Doadja likely keeps an eye on him. No political activity has been detected, so this monitoring appears to have been minimal, just watching to see if he does become active. He has been able to go back and forth to Doadja to visit his family without any issues.

Although Lare has kept a low profile with respect to politics, he has a group of friends with whom he discusses the inequities and nastiness of life in Doadja, but he is otherwise quite careful. He has never expressed openly a desire to become leader, but his education and his natural leadership skills means that there could be others who see him as a potential future national level leader. If the situation improved in Doadja, it is likely that he would return there without hesitation. What he wants the most is to have Doadja run by a reasonable, incorrupt government that will start providing the basics of health care and education to the people. He is less concerned about democracy than about effective delivery of government services and a sharing of the country's wealth. His whole upbringing was morally focused on ensuring that everyone has a basic level of health care, education, and employment. These goals are extremely important to him.

His writings in various academic journals suggest that he seethes inwardly about the current situation in Doadja. He quotes the Dalai Lama in one article, "It is not enough to be compassionate; you must act." Lare himself has been quoted in the press as saying, "we all aspire to better days."

I'm thinking that Lare is someone I should meet. I filled in Matt and Dan and told them that I would fly to Senegal and try to meet with him to cautiously feel out his level of interest in our proposal.

I needed to create a believable pretense for going to Senegal to meet with Lare. I came up with the idea that Global Affairs had asked me to conduct an overview of the security situation in Doadja, and I needed some perspectives from outside the country. I used Lare's email address at the university and asked for a meeting. He responded the next day, indicating that he wasn't in a knowledgeable position to discuss security, but that if I wanted more background or context about Doadja, he would be happy to meet with me. I suggested a morning meeting to occur three days later, and then I started to line up my trip. Of course, once again it was personal, not official, so I took a leave from work for five days.

I flew through New York on Delta's direct flight to Dakar, breezed through the airport, and then had a car and driver take me the four and a half hours' road trip to Saint Louis, Senegal. It felt good to be back in Africa with some time to look around as we drove north. I had checked into a nice hotel in Saint Louis, not far from the university, and went over to meet with Lare the next morning.

"Dr. Lare, I'm Nadeem Nawaz," I said, extending my hand. "It's a pleasure to meet you."

A welcoming smile and handshake greeted me. I know that people sometimes think that I look like a university professor, but Lare is an even better fit to the stereotype. An elegant north African face, tortoise shell-rimmed glasses, and a casual smile all fit the profile. Although still not even middle-aged at thirty-seven, his face had an intelligent, experienced look.

"Mr. Nawaz, I understand that you are seeking more information about the situation in Doadja. As I indicated in my email, I am happy to help, but I may not be the best person. As you may know, I have lived outside the country for some time. I try to keep up with news, and through my personal contacts, but because of the nature of the government there, everyone is cautious about discussing any subjects dealing with security or politics, or even poverty or health care."

"I am sure you know the basic, public facts about my unfortunate country. Public education is almost non-existent, more than eighty percent of the population lives on less than two dollars per day, and life expectancy is incredibly low. Other than a few private hospitals like those that my parents established, most of the public has almost no access to basic health care. There are very few African countries in a worse state. The real tragedy is that, nominally, the country is wealthy with a substantial oil industry and some other valuable minerals."

"I do know that, Dr. Lare, but are there any plans to improve the situation?"

"Under the current government, no, but many people know what is needed. The country needs a ten-year plan to build the basics, starting with education and health, using revenue from the oil concessions to invest in the people. To develop other elements that will raise employment levels, provide some dignity to people, and diversify the economy will take even longer. Any change will take time because the starting point is so low."

"You seem to have a vision for the country."

"I am sure that I am not the only one. It is a ridiculous situation for a country with such high revenue to be in such a state."

"Dr. Lare, I need to be more open with you about the real reason I am here. There are several of us in Canada who believe that it may be possible to organize a change of government in Doadja, and we are looking for potential Doadjan leadership to collaborate with us to effect this change."

"Mr. Nadeem, let's walk."

Lare stood up and led me out of the office and into a square on the campus.

"Mr. Nawaz, before you arrived, I checked out your background, and even your picture, to be sure that I was really meeting with you today and that you were indeed a senior official in the Canadian government. You need to appreciate that even raising the subject that you have could endanger me?"

"Please call me Nadeem. May I call you Rafael?"

"Of course."

"Rafael, we are aware of the risks, but we believe that the need for change is pressing and that you are the best person to lead a changed country."

"Why is Canada interested in this, and why now?"

"Well, I am here in a private role, not on behalf of the government of Canada. Why now, is because I have a Canadian friend that Obissey is holding at Wailing Island without charge and without trial."

"So, this is a group of Canadian individuals that believe they can overthrow Obissey? I don't know whether to laugh or admire the sheer audacity of it. Who is this Canadian?"

"James Mackenzie."

"James is well-known to all in Doadja. Do you know what happened?"

"He had some sort of business disagreement with the President over money. I met with Obissey and there was nothing that indicated he is prepared to release James. He seems to want to make an example of him, so that nobody else tries to shortchange him."

"He's a good example, I would say, Nadeem. Everyone in Doadja will know eventually that the famous arms dealer and President's business partner is in jail and unlikely to ever be seen again. Mr. Mackenzie may be a friend of yours but I would like to see him gone from Doadja. His partnership with the president is simply a source of evil. Obissey issues false end-user certificates to JaMAC and that company supplies arms everywhere in Africa, and even elsewhere, using those bogus documents. Since the arrest of Victor Bout in 2008, James Mackenzie is arguably the leading illegal weapons dealer in the world. He is highly active on an ongoing basis in Africa today, including in the Congo, in Libya, and in the Sahel."

"I agree, Rafael, that James has become an unsavoury character, but there is a group of us that feel that the death sentence that is inevitable with being entombed on Wailing Island is not the appropriate punishment."

"Perhaps, but the more important issue is how is this related to any type of change of government in Doadja, and how can a group of foreigners successfully undertake what would amount to a coup? I say coup, because Obissey will not leave willingly under any circumstances."

"Let me answer both of those questions, Rafael. As the first step, we tried to get James released simply through foreign interest and negotiation. That was, as you now know, unsuccessful. We explored bribery, and even a jailbreak, but neither of those options seemed feasible."

"The idea of a coup occurred to us because the more we looked into the situation in your country, the more we realized that some sort of action to help the people there is long overdue. Because our group is ex-military, or serving military, our assessment is that a coup is feasible because it hasn't been attempted before in Doadja. In effect, we would be achieving two important things; freeing James, and more importantly, freeing your country at the same time. As you know, there is a complacency at the top that makes all elements of state security vulnerable. In addition, the loyalty of the army is suspect, and Obissey is only kept in place by a small leadership group that wields the threat of Presidential Guard action against any dissent. In addition, Sabi Issa, James' number two man, has an extensive mercenary network that is still active, and because of the trade of JaMAC, he has access to a stockpile of weapons."

"Speaking of JaMAC, Nadeem, if Obissey is angry with Mackenzie, why hasn't he seized the company?"

"Because Sabi keeps making large monthly payments. Seizing the company would cut off that flow of money and leave the government with a bunch of weapons that it doesn't need. So far, JaMAC isn't seen as a threat. Rather, it's regarded as a cash cow."

"Nadeem, you do know that a similar coup was attempted in Equatorial Guinea in 2004 and failed before it was even put into action."

"Yes, but the famous Wonga Coup was an embarrassment. Trusting Mugabe was a critical error. Also, its security was so laughably bad that I think every security service in the world was aware of the pending coup well in advance."

"And this will be different?"

"Absolutely. We don't need outside support from another country – European, African, or Canada, for that matter. We don't have any contact with security agencies and we will not involve them. There are many countries that would be happy to see Obissey gone, but involving any of them would simply lower the chances of success."

"Tell me, Nadeem, what would be my role in this if I agreed?"

"You would arrive in Doadja at the very moment that the coup removes Obissey and go directly to the government communications centre, which would be under our control. From there, you would announce the change of government, ask the army to stand down, announce a truth and reconciliation commission to deal with crimes by the Presidential Guard, and then outline your plans for a better country."

"And what if the attempt to remove Obissey fails?"

"The jet that would have brought you to Doadja would immediately turn around and return to its origin. Only a small group of us would know that you were the person who was being introduced as the new President. In fact, there would only be four people in Doadja at the time of the coup who would know that. It is likely that if the coup fails, you would never be identified as having been a part of it."

"You make it sound risk-free for me, which I very much doubt. I would need to see a detailed plan on how this would work before I could possibly agree. Failure would result in murderous attacks on all contenders, wherever they are in the world. The complacency you referred to would be over."

"Agreed, let me get back to you with a detailed plan, Rafael. Let's talk about how to communicate. We are exploring completely secure communications, but in the meantime, we will be using the chat function inside a computer game to communicate. I also have a list with me that I will give you today that has substitute names for various people and places so that, even if someone happens to access the game dialog, it will not provide a clear picture of what we are dealing with."

"And the game?"

"It is Civilization VI; you will need to acquire a license. We are proposing that you log in every day at ten p.m. and join a game that we will set up together. We will play for a few minutes progressing the game, then put messages into the chat. I expect we will be replacing that with a more secure communication method before any action is taken. Incidentally, make sure you use your laptop to communicate with us, and avoid your mobile. Let's assume that Obissey has his people keeping an eye on you."

"Okay, Nadeem, but please understand that agreeing to go along with this communication does not mean that I agree to the coup. I will need to see the plan before I can take another step."

"Fine, Rafael, I will be the only one that communicates with you, and only two other people in Canada know that we are talking. No one in Doadja is involved in these discussions."

Chapter 11.
Team Plan - April

As soon as Nadeem returned from Senegal, he sent an email to Matt, Dan, Max, and Alida suggesting that the gang of five meet at his place.

When they got together, Nadeem started the conversation.

"First, let me bring you up-to-date on Rafael Lare. I know that my meeting with him was brief, but I believe he is the right person. He has a vision for Doadja that could be a substantial change for the country. As you might expect, he is very wary of our concept. After all, it's a coup orchestrated by a group of Canadians. That said, he won't give us a decision until he sees a detailed plan."

"On the plus side, he agrees with our perspective that the country is ready for change and it is a likely candidate for a takeover. Security measures are light, driven by years of complacency under Obissey without any significant challenges. There is a fearful population that understands that they are being screwed by him but believe that they have no alternative. Lare believes that the army would readily change allegiance once it was clear that Obissey was removed. One concern that I have is that Lare may be too soft due to his strong sense of morality. When he sees the details of our plan, he may see that it is feasible, but still be uncomfortable with the possible fatalities that may occur."

"But I think that we would all rather deal with someone who tends to be too moral, than a replacement that is as bad as Obissey."

"We have work to do. We need to develop a coup plan that is sufficiently detailed to present to Lare and Sabi. Sabi will be critical on this, he will need to do all the heavy lifting – lining up the mercenary team, sourcing weapons, and acting as point man on the coup itself. We can be deeply involved in the planning, but the coup cannot appear to be led by white foreigners."

"Dan, I would like you to take the lead from here on with the planning aspect. I will continue to function as liaison with Lare, and if it is easy to cloak our intent, I want to return to Doadja to meet with Sabi."

With that, I handed it over to Dan.

"Okay, Nadeem. We can start tonight, but this may take a few days. Before I begin, though, I would like to talk about security. There is at least one well-known spectacular failure of a small country coup of this type – the attempted coup in Equatorial Guinea in 2004. The key to its unravelling was extremely poor security, so that what was going to happen was known to many governments well in advance of the actual coup. Indeed, several of them may have been peripherally involved. If you weren't aware of this, I suggest that you check it out – look up the Wonga Coup. Nadeem, I know that you are aware of it."

"We have numerous advantages over that attempt. First, if we can access the financial resources of James or JaMAC, we don't need outside financial involvement – which was one of the leakiest areas in 2004. Second, we are unlikely to need external sources for weapons, if JaMAC has a weapons pipeline in place, and a significant amount stored in Doadja."

"Our other security weak spots are the mercenaries and our need to communicate with Sabi and Lare. We will need to keep all the mercs in the dark as to the potential country target, the date, etc., until just before the actual coup. Fortunately, several of the neighbouring countries have a flow of mercenaries in and out because they are being used routinely to guard mines for diamonds, copper, or coltan. We can use that as a guise over a period of some weeks while assembling our teams outside the country."

"In terms of comms, I will explore extremely secure communication options for the lead up and the coup, but in the short-term, we will all play Civilization VI as we already discussed."

"You all know the key targets for the coup. My proposed approach is a simultaneous 'shock and awe' approach to these actions. They will happen all at once, mostly during a period of minutes, with the tail dragging on for an hour at most."

"I know that this will require more resources, but my impression is that Sabi can assemble sufficient resources. The trick will be getting them into Doadja just in time, and not before."

"In terms of 'risk of failure,' the highest would be a failure to assassinate Obissey. This could happen for a few reasons: early warning through some leak of information, he is not in the palace when we expect him to be there, or because the Presidential Guard repels us. The next highest risk factor would be the failure to take out the army and the Guard leadership. We need the chaos of that vacuum at the top to give us time to get the new president in place. The third risk would be a failure to contain the army on the island. Even if we dispose of the leadership, if they can easily disperse off the island, we will lose control of the situation rapidly. The final risk factor would be the failure to block and contain the off-duty Presidential Guard in the area on the edge of the city."

"The basis of the whole strategy that I have drafted is to get the message out that Obissey is dead, along with a clear message that Lare is in place in a demonstrably live format, like live interviews on TV, radio, and the Internet. This must be done before any real opposition can develop. It is also based on the premise that the only enthusiastic opposition will be from the Presidential Guard, and the bulk of fatalities will be in the Guard. We want to give the actual army every chance to not take serious action."

"With all this in mind, I developed a first cut at timing and people. I think you will need to take a few hours to review, comment, and improve upon it, but let me first highlight a few points."

At that juncture, Dan opened his backpack and handed out a sheet containing a table to each of the others.

Draft Action Plan

Action	Day	Start Time	End Time	Leader	Personnel
				Resources	
Weapons, Vehicles, explosives in Place	-4			Sabi	6
National Park Team across border	-3			Sabi	28
Liquor Trucks team to Doala	-2			Sabi	23
Fit out Bridge/Palace Trucks	-2			Dan	6
Guard Ambush Team Road Work	0	8:00	18:30	Max	
New Pres Flight to Doula	0	17:10	18:40	Alida	
Disable/Seize aircraft	0	18:00	18:25	Alida	4
Sieze Tower	0	18:30	18:40	Alida	4
Control Communications Centre	0	18:45	18:58	Dan	8
Bridge trucks to Bridge/Activate	0	18:40	19:00	DM3	2
Take out Guard and Army Leaders	0	18:50	19:00	DM2	4
Sieze Comm Centre	0	19:00	19:03	Dan	4
Close off Bridge	0	19:00	19:04	DM3	6
Palace Frontal Assault	0	19:00	19:06	DM1	5
Take out Pres	0	19:00	19:15	Sabi	12
Release taped TV Interview New Pres	0	19:06	19:20	Dan	
New Pres to Comm Centre	0	19:10	19:20	Alida	2
New Pres Live Interview		19:20	20:00	Alida	
Deny Access Pres Guard Off-Duty		19:10	19:40	Max	16

"Before you ask questions, let me take you through the timing that I am proposing:

- We will need forty to fifty trained personnel. Of that group, we will require at least six of them that speak Doadjan. That team needs to include a high-voltage electrician, one or two air traffic controllers, and one or two demolition specialists. The exact number will become clear as our detailed plan evolves.
- Starting a week or so before the coup, the mercenaries will individually travel to adjacent countries, using their

mining security role as a cover. They will, of course, be unarmed. We will arm them in Doadja.

- Mobilization will start at zero day minus four. We will need that time to prepare a few specialized vehicles, setting them up with shaped charges to deny access to the army and to breach the palace. Also, four days prior to the coup, we need a go/no-go decision point to be sure that all the weapons and materials are where we need them to be. This will also need to include the use of secure satcom, although the use of this will need to be limited to the day of the coup, so as not to attract any advance attention from Doadja, the neighbouring countries, or the US/UK/French security agencies.

- The national park stretches from the edge of Nambi to the borders of two adjacent countries. I am proposing that, three days in advance of coup day, at least half the assault team will cross into Doadja on foot and move from the border to a pickup point in the park, two kilometres from the border. This park is essentially empty. There are no tourists because Doadja is in such bad repute. There are no locals living in the park. The only traffic is occasional hunters, illegally seeking bush meat.

- Two days before the coup, the remaining twenty-three members of the assault team will assemble at a designated pickup point, ready for two trucks to pick them up on the day of the assault. We will need to find a location, where an assembly like this will not attract attention, something like an abandoned mill. They will be unarmed at this point. Individually, there will be nothing suspicious about them. We will be able to move them across the border easily, hidden in JaMAC trucks that do frequent runs to take wine and liquor to Obissey's palace.

- We will be using the two days inside JaMAC's warehouse and compound to fit out our vehicles, arm-up, and train/practice for two critical steps – getting the two trucks parked side-by-side for the bridge, and then getting the assault team into the palace.

- With respect to the Presidential Guard base, we would arrange a fake roadwork project on the highway between the Guard base and the edge of town, to enable us to mine the road and establish an ambush point. This road work will start on the morning of the coup. I believe that even though we will have shut down the Internet, radio, etc., the base will still get a radio message from the palace that they are under attack and that the entire base will assemble into a convoy. This is where the major firepower will be needed. The Guard will know that they are completely dependent on Obissey's survival and will fight. We need to take out that convoy. They have old soviet LAVs so we will need to be able to destroy those while they are in convoy on that road. We will use a combination of IEDs and RPGs with follow up small arms fire and mines.

- I am proposing an early evening assault for several reasons. Firstly, Obissey is almost always in the palace at that time having dinner with his wife. Secondly, heavier traffic at that time will help us delay any movement by the off-duty Presidential Guard. I specifically am not proposing a late-night attack, because the personal security element in Doadja is so bad that by about nine p.m., the streets are virtually empty, and the movement of trucks or large groups of people will immediately attract attention.

- The real action will start at 18:00, with a lot of activities happening in parallel – at 18:00 air force guards at the military hangar at the airport will be silenced and the two jets disabled. At 18:20 we will seize the tower at the airport and staff it with our own people. Both the hangar operation and the tower takeover must be done silently and without setting off any alarms, because these actions will happen up to an hour before the full kickoff.

- On coup day, we will need a business jet to bring Lare to Doadja and to land just at the time of coup. That should be chartered in Senegal, because sending James' plane may arouse suspicion. He will depart from a nearby country to arrive at the airport in Nambi at 18:40. One of the team already at the airport disabling aircraft and seizing the tower will take Lare to the government comms centre.

- We need to have control of the communications centre before 19:00 when the palace and bridge attacks will occur. This will happen in two stages – first, we will cut off the power and the supplementary standby generator power, then we will take the building. This takeover needs to be done rapidly and silently; we need to avoid any alarm going out by phone, radio, TV, or Internet.

- Also, before 19:00, we will need to neutralize the army and Guard leadership silently in their homes. Sabi will know where they live. This is a small city in a small country.

- In the last twenty minutes before 19:00, all the teams will be in motion – the bridge trucks will be enroute to block the bridge at zero hour, the palace bomb truck and team will be enroute to the palace, and the Guard attack team will be moving from road work to ambush positions.

- At 19:00 the shitstorm breaks out. We will almost simultaneously block the bridge, deal with the Guard soldiers in front of the palace, breach the palace, and then broadcast a taped message from Lare on all comms channels.

- In the following twenty minutes, the plan has control shifting completely to the new President. He will arrive at the comms building and conduct live interviews to show that he is in the country, and in control. Simultaneous with that, the assault teams will be denying access to the city by the army and the Guard. If all goes to plan, the Guard will be destroyed and the army will be sufficiently discouraged that the messages from Lare will convince them to stand down."

Max interjected,

"Great pace, what about weapons and supplies?"

Dan continued,

"In terms of weapons we need a lot of short-barrel automatic weapons, for working indoors. We need silenced handguns for work at the airport and at the homes of the Guard and army leadership. We also need some heavier weapons such as RPGs to deny access to the bridge from the island, and to neutralize movement by the off-duty Presidential Guard. For both the army area and the Guard base, the concept is to go big on fire power to increase the apparent size of our assault group and to destroy the will to fight. I have developed a list of what I think we need and will pass it to Sabi."

"I have also taken a first cut at the other resources we will need. We will require at least six trucks, and in sufficient time to ensure that we can modify them. That will take two days. We can undertake the mod work inside one of the JaMAC warehouses. My idea for the bridge is to back two trucks onto the bridge side-by-side, and then blow the whole rear wheel and suspensions off them so that they become immovable in the short-term. We will fill the trucks with gravel to reduce the chance of, say, an armoured vehicle pushing them out of the way. The bridge from the island has no sidewalks and two trucks will completely block the bridge, making even pedestrian access difficult. As an extra fail-safe measure, I am proposing to have steel plating welded underneath each truck, down to almost road level, to prevent troops from crawling under them to get into the city if the charges fail for some reason. For the palace, my idea is to rig a truck with shaped charges at the tailgate area. We would back it up to the palace wall and blow a hole into the palace large enough for the attack team to quickly get through."

"Of course, over the next day, access to the island will be enabled, James and other political prisoners will be freed, and any of the Canadian team that is in-country will leave with James on the bizjet to return to Canada. Questions?"

Max had another question,

"Dan, you are bringing in the assault teams in two groups, but there are seven targets. How are you breaking out the teams to get the six individual target teams in place? Who is doing what?"

"Good question. As you might suspect, I have already given it some thought. We will assemble the teams when we are all together on the day before the coup. You, Alida, Sabi, and I will lead four of the teams. Sabi has indicated that he has three experienced Doadjan mercenaries that will lead the others."

Nadeem jumped in,

"Dan, I thought that you had originally said Alida would not be directly involved in the action?"

"I did, Nadeem, but she changed my mind. She wants to be involved and the fact that she fits into the local scene better than the rest of us can be used to our advantage."

Dan added,

"Max, the most dynamic issue will be the firefight to shut down the bulk of the off-duty Guard attempting to come to the palace. I am proposing that you lead this team. It needs demolition expertise and a cool head in an intense short-range engagement. We need to be sure that your team also has a senior guy who speaks Doadjan."

Alida then asked,

"Dan, it sounds like the Presidential Guard will be the key problem, although we are guessing that the army will not put up an enthusiastic fight. Is there any kind of a plan to reduce the Guard's commitment to Obissey, beyond destroying them?

"No, Sabi and I don't see any other option. We will need to decimate them, and I believe we can take out fifty to eighty percent of their force before they surrender, but also, as soon as Lare is in the comm centre, one part of his message will be to set up a Truth and Reconciliation Commission and to advise everyone to stand down and avoid vengeance. I'm not sure it will be credible, but it may help."

It was Nadeem's turn to grill Dan:

"Matt and I are here not only in the role of helping James, but now as fathers of two of the team that will be at risk if this unravels. Tell us about your ideas for extraction if the plan fails. What if Obissey is not killed, what if the large Guard group gets to the palace, what if the army stays loyal and fights its way off the island?"

Dan responded,

"Failure, Nadeem? That hurts. Sabi has at least one soviet BMP-3 stored at the warehouse. If the palace team fails to gain entry or fails to kill Obissey, or if the off-duty guard breaks through our barrier, the three of us in-country and Sabi will use that vehicle to pick us up and get us to the airport. The four of us will use the bizjet to depart. It will all happen very quickly, so we will still control the tower and nearby countries won't have closed borders."

"In the case of the mercenaries, if we fail to breach the palace and make the kill, then that team will be lost. If the Guard breaks through our ambush, then the residual group will take the trucks through the national park. We will have cut up the Guard so badly at that point that they are unlikely to follow, at least until the next day. For mercenaries at other locations, they will need to use the cars that are there to head for the national park, where we will establish a fall-back pickup point where the trucks can pick them up to take them to the border."

Matt commented:

"Dan, by making the coup not much more than an hour long, you provide lots of opportunity for those less than enthusiastic about Obissey to sit back and do nothing. The weakness that I see is the absolute need for secrecy throughout. The mercenaries cannot know the destination, the timing, or even how many of them there are until just prior to first movement. Any event like one of the adjacent countries noticing a strange build up of mine security people, or any breach of our communications by one of the sophisticated US, UK, or France intelligence agencies will be fatal, because the assault teams are small. And that could be fatal for the Canadian team because they may be already in-country when Doadja is made aware of the attempt. We will need a go/no-go point when the mercenaries are already in position to start into Doadja, but the Canadian team is still here. We also need highly secure comms between us, and particularly with Sabi. We will be dependent on Sabi. We need to assume that Obissey has had Sabi under surveillance since James was arrested. In a perfect world, our electronic comms would be minimal, and so diverse in methods and so encrypted, that if we become aware that someone has detected the coup in advance, there will not be a trail leading back to us."

"One key trail that we will need to think through carefully is the money. I know that we will not need to access outside funds if we can deal with JaMAC accounts, but the mercenaries will need some form of up-front payment for some of their fees plus their travel expenses."

Alida interjected:

"If the coup is successful, then the follow-up completion payments can come from the new government and will not be a big concern. I will need to work with Sabi on this, because JaMAC likely has some devious links into a lot of the other African countries because of the nature of its business. If we can use those, we can cloak the payments."

Dan continued:

"If you all think the idea is workable and the risks manageable, I need to return to Doadja and meet with Sabi. I need to get his input to further develop the plan and to flesh out details re the skills we need from the mercs and the exact gear that will be required. There are several essential elements that still need to be lined up with Sabi's help."

"We need a floorplan of the palace, or at least a reasonable sketch of the layout. We will use that information to determine the best location where we can blast a hole to gain access. My understanding so far is that although there is a courtyard at the front side of the palace, on the other three sides, the building wall is also the perimeter wall. Once through that wall, the team will be inside the palace."

"We also need to finalize the entry details for the comm centre and the airport tower. Some questions still need to be answered. For example, do we bribe individuals who are already open to oppose the government? How do we identify those people? Do we use silent cutting tools? In both areas we need to be in the building before the people inside are aware that we are there."

"Ali, you raised the money issue, I think you will need to go to Doadja and work out that issue with Sabi. We must be sure that we have what we need. I will pin this down with Sabi and confirm if he agrees that this is needed."

"Nadeem, you need to meet with Lare, walk him through this plan, and get him locked down. If he isn't all in, we cannot proceed. His confirmation of the unwillingness of most of the population to fight for Obissey is also important."

"Everyone, my idea here is that the slower we move, the more risk of failure. For one thing, James is fading away in that prison. I propose that if anyone has better ideas or wants to withdraw, they do so before the end of day Thursday. Otherwise, we will be off to Doadja to flesh out the plan. Of course, there will be another chance to review and finalize it when we return."

Max smiled and commented:

"I know that rescuing James is the ultimate goal here, but man, for me this potential close combat for a good cause is living the dream."

Smiles and nods from all around the table.

Chapter 12.
Dan - April – May

Thursday evening, I logged into Civilization VI and after fifteen minutes of playing, texted Sabi in the chat function.

Sabi, I will be in Dakar Sunday. If you happen to be there, we could talk about strategies for the game. I will be at the Novotel Dakar.

After an affirmative response from Sabi, I booked a flight through New York to Dakar and reserved a room at the four-star hotel. The airport in Dakar is, of course, more efficient than the airport in Doadja. I was through immigration, customs, and out the door in about forty minutes. I grabbed a taxi to take me to the hotel. I knew it wasn't far, but it still took a half-hour because the route was right through downtown. The Novotel is on the coast near the port, and I was taken to a nice room overlooking the waterfront.

On Sunday, Sabi came up to my room.

"Hello, Sabi, good to see you again. As you might expect, I have a lot to update you on, but I suggest we move outdoors and work by the pool. I have booked a cabana."

I led Sabi down to the pool area overlooking the ocean. Although there was a small road between the hotel and the waterfront, the traffic was light, so it was quiet enough, and comfortable in the shade.

"Sabi, I just feel more secure out of the hotel room. I have a plan to discuss with you and it is dramatic. Absolute secrecy on this will be critical, as you know. After we were together in Doadja, our thinking took a different direction. Simply put, I think with your help and resources we can cause regime change in Doadja. I developed a fairly detailed plan and then ran it by the group of Canadians at my end to see their reactions. You and your old network will be critical to the success of this, so we really need to work through it together. I brought printed material for you to review on resources, material, etc. I will need to take it back from you before we leave, however and will send you an encrypted version. You cannot fly back to Doadja with these notes in your backpack."

"Your thinking doesn't surprise me, Dan; I have had some of the same thoughts."

"But first, Sabi, what is the current situation in Doadja?"

"No change about James, and no additional information. I keep the business going and continue to make payments into Obissey's accounts for his 'share.' I have also been distributing any weapons, ammo, etc. that we have to various sites that I don't think the government is aware of, just in case Obissey decides to simply seize everything. I don't think that will happen as long as the cash keeps flowing. He doesn't know the business well enough to have someone keep it going if he messes it up."

"Any change in the mood of the public – any shift that would threaten Obissey?"

"No, you know this has gone on forever, right? Between Obissey and his dad, there has been no change for so long that people have given up all hope."

I handed Sabi the notes, tables, and sketches that I had put together. As he started reviewing them, I called over the pool server and ordered coffee.

"Take your time, Sabi, we can have coffee while you look at the information."

He studied the documents carefully, putting them face down on the table when the coffee came, and then continuing. After about fifteen minutes, he spoke:

"Dan, overall, it seems like your plan is trying to do a lot with very few people. Absolute surprise will be critical. If the government or the big Western countries detect any elements of this in advance, we are screwed. The Presidential Guard will simply staff up all the critical points and be ready. Even the army could be brought into play.”

“Agreed, this is all built on secrecy. Do you see a problem with that?”

“Doadja is not really sophisticated. I assume that Obissey’s people are monitoring Doadjan phones, with Pegasus on anyone’s phone they are interested in, including mine. But if I use burners, we can avoid any penetration there. The high-risk element for me will be the mercenaries. We need to be sure that once in Doadja, they have no cell phones. That will mean searching every one of them. People these days are so attached to their phones.”

“What about the Canadian end? Any risk elements there?” asked Sabi.

“No, I don’t see any. The only people aware of this would be Nadeem, Matt, Alida, me, and Max.”

“And who is Max?”

“Maxime Lapcyre is a colleague of mine in the special forces. I have added him because he is tops in kinetic ops. We call him Absolute, for Absolute Max. He’s one of those special characters who thrives when the heat is on. He is an experienced combat officer and I want him to be part of the team.”

“Dan, I believe you said before that there will be no government agencies, no external funding?”

“That’s right, we don’t need or want any government involvement. Not Canadian, Brit, American, or French. Nobody. And all financing will have to be internal. Essentially, JaMAC will need to finance this.”

“That may be a problem because I don’t have access to James’ bank accounts.”

“Yes, we must get access. If we cannot finance this internally, it cannot proceed. Way too much of a risk of leaks, otherwise. Let’s come back to that, I think we have a solution for that one.”

“Your coup material doesn’t say who would be taking on the presidency.”

"We have talked to Rafael Lare, and if he can be convinced this is feasible, he will be the man."

"Hmm, an interesting choice. I know that he has been low profile, but the public sees his whole family as ethical and committed to the country. The government is certainly monitoring him, so there is another risk element there in terms of possible leakage. But with him, it looks feasible. It's the breathtaking pace that makes it look interesting to me. The idea of moving quickly enough to discourage an organized response makes it seem possible. The army is hopeless, and if we can create the impression of a done deal, they will quickly stand down."

"Dan, if we do manage to pull this off, can we mobilize the army afterwards to round up any leftover Presidential Guard, prevent looting; all that kind of thing?"

"I'm not sure. There's no way to really tell, but my best guess is yes, particularly with Lare in place."

"Obviously, you will be the key element of this, Sabi, in many ways. Firstly, you are Doadjan. This cannot be, or look like, a coup by a bunch of white guy foreigners. The leadership on the ground must be local. In your mercenary network, are there other Doadjans that could be involved?"

"Yes, when I left the Congo, I brought out a couple of guys with me. They are now very experienced and interested in change in Doadja."

"And, Sabi, we would of course need to rely on you for the weapons, ammo, and all the related materiel and logistics."

"That is what I am good at. We are in an excellent spot to start with, I had a lot of gear in storage that was being shipped out to various groups in the Congo in small loads. When I found out that Obissey had arrested James, I distributed all of that to various locations in Doadja, just in case Obissey moved against the company.

"Dan, I need to mention that the weapons we deal in are mostly Russian or Chinese because they are a lot less intrusive on end-user certificates than Western countries. Your weapons list is specific, re MP5's and the other weapons."

"Treat the weapons on my list as examples. For instance, when I specify MP5s, I really mean short barrel automatic assault weapons. We need the suppressors where indicated, because we will need silence in the early attacks to avoid alarms going out."

"We have a lot of AKs, and handguns with silencers. What we do have in terms of Western weapons are some 50 cals and heavy sniper weapons. We don't have Western light antitank weapons."

"Not a problem, Sabi, we will figure out a workaround on that. The goal with those is to take out Guard vehicles entering the city in a way that totally wipes out the troops on board. We will not have enough firepower to deal with large numbers of Guard troops if they can offload them from a damaged vehicle. The first strike must take out the vehicles and their occupants – up to five vehicles, and as close to concurrently as possible."

"Okay, Dan. IEDs and RPGs will do the job if we can pin down the location. I have the experienced guys to do that. Things are so poorly-run here that a fake road crew will not even attract attention from security people."

"Max will be leading the attack on the Presidential Guard. We can leave some of the logistical details with him. He will need a Doadjan-speaking team leader with him to interact with anyone that comes along while they are setting up the ambush."

"Sabi, can you get the vehicles that I have listed without a problem?"

"Dan, you will laugh. In addition to JaMAC trucks, we often bribe the army to lend us trucks to use in border runs to bring in liquor for Obissey and for various high-priced help."

"That's great – those trucks just kind of cruise past the customs posts?"

"Well, not just drive through, they have to stop so that the customs officers can offload a case of whiskey for themselves."

"Sabi, there are some other things I am going to need help with as soon as possible. It is important that we get palace floorplans or a sketch of the palace layout."

"Floorplans may not be possible, but I think we can develop a reasonable sketch. There are quite a few retired palace staff that may remember the layout for a small bribe."

"Okay, but keep that group as small as possible, and with people you know you can trust. We don't want anyone wondering why you need the sketch."

"Next, we need a location to modify the trucks for the bridge and the palace wall breach."

"Not a problem, Dan. JaMAC has lots of warehouse space, including one that is currently not in use at all. None of our staff are there. We can set it up so that only those people you approve, plus selected mercs, are on site. Tell me more about how these trucks will be kitted out."

"The two bridge trucks must be critically disabled side-by-side on the bridge. Ideally, we want to blow off the wheels in a way that brings the trucks down flat on the bridge so that army soldiers cannot cross the bridge by crawling under the trucks. I believe that the two trucks will fill the space so tightly that we will need to remove the windshields so that the two drivers can escape over the hoods once the trucks are in-place and disabled. Oh, and they need to have enough weight on-board to prevent the army from using an LAV to push them off. I suggest filling them with gravel. I assume that the army will eventually find a way to deal with them, the critical thing is to give us an hour to take control."

"The palace truck needs to have a frame added below the rear end, down low, as close to road level as is feasible without it dragging enroute to the palace. The idea is that we will attach the linear shaped charges in a large doorway configuration, and that needs to come down lower than a normal truck bed. Because we can't waste time climbing over a piece of wall on the way in, the blasted opening must be low enough not to slow down our troops. Timing of seconds may be critical there."

"Okay, again, that shouldn't be a problem. We can weld on a drop piece. In fact, some of our trucks already have part of that in place to support a lower bumper."

"A couple of other things, Sabi. Can you and I do a waterfront wander tomorrow? We need to find locations for our team to set up to suppress movement off the island. We will block the bridge, but my idea is to use a combination of 50 cal sniper fire, and LAW or RPG fire, to discourage any exit from the prison complex entrance. This will also create the impression that they are up against a much larger force. My idea is to pour on the fire power to give us that initial period until we have seized all the key elements of the government and are sure that Lare is in control."

"Also, I know there will be an alert team at the hangar for those two fighter jets. Through bribery, observation, or whatever, we will need to know how many and where. I suspect there will be about ten, including pilots, support crew, and a couple of sentries."

"Next, Sabi, is the money issue. I have estimated that we will need over fifty soldiers, including some experienced leaders. You will have a better idea than I do as to how much that will cost. Does JaMAC have the funds to pull this off, and do you have mechanisms to pay these funds? My thinking is that the mercs will need an up-front payment and some form of guaranteed payment to go to them or their families after the coup. At least the front-end payment will have to come from JaMAC, we don't want to bring in outside money. I figure the post-coup payment can be made by the new government as a thank you note."

"I see, Dan. JaMAC has the money as far as I know. We have been stock-piling money for years, but accessing it is a different thing. I am James' COO. My job was primarily to work the African end of deals, then to get the weapons out to our customers. James kept the money issues close to his vest. I believe we have offshore accounts in a bunch of locations, but I don't know the details."

"Sabi. I am going to ask Alida to come over and work with you to try and access these funds and to work out how to distribute the front-end payments under the radar. I will email her tonight and get her here asap."

"Alida is Nadeem's daughter, as you know, but that is not why I want to bring her over. Since she left the army, she obtained an MBA and a CPA and has been working as a forensic accountant with KPMG for some years now. If anyone can locate and get into James' bank accounts, it will be her. As a further benefit, Alida's mom is Rwandan, so she won't stand out in a crowd over here. She also speaks English, French, and Spanish."

"Sounds good, Dan. I will give her access to whatever I can. It is critical that we get into some of the big accounts because we are going to have a lot of expenses."

"Ali is fierce when she gets her teeth into a challenge. Unless James has some unusual computer skills and exceptional secrecy smarts, she will likely be able to figure out the accounts and passwords. From you, she will need accounts to which she can transfer this money."

"I already have a plan for that, Dan. I am going to create several accounts that sound so much like the real mining companies, that the small banks I am using will assume that they are from the legitimate mining operations. I already have someone creating the bogus paperwork. I am going to use these companies to 'hire' the mercenaries as mine security guards. I've named them Kumba Minerals and Northam Precious Metals."

"Good thinking, Sabi. The last thing I need from you is to know how much time you need to line up your mercs. How long until we know that we have the numbers we need, and how long until they could be in-place as fake mine guards? That looks like the critical timeline, and the sooner we move the better."

"I will need to get back to you, Dan, on both of those times. My first guess is about ten days to confirm the people. I already have active networks with these guys because of our business. Some of them are "retail" customers. As soon as I have the group pinned down, I will be able to give you a firm estimate on the second point. Some of the guys will need visas for the pre-positioning countries and we may need to create a whole fake mine security operation for that."

"Understood."

"Dan, if I can round up the mercs I want, I think we will have a killer team."

"Great, keep checking the Civ VI game and get me the palace sketch as soon as you can."

"Will do, Dan. Once I have it, I will travel out of Doadja and use a burner phone in a nearby country to send you a jpg or pdf."

Chapter 13.
Alida - April – May

I have travelled a lot in my job at KPMG, and of course I did a tour in Afghanistan, but Africa was a new adventure for me, even though I am part Rwandan. Too bad it was Doadja instead of South Africa or Botswana. Doadja is really the armpit of Africa, with almost no tourists and no decent tourist infrastructure. So, there I was, at the infamous Continental Hotel, with its algae-filled swimming pool.

In the morning Sabi was there to pick me up.

"You must be Alida?"

"Sabi?"

"Yes, welcome to Doadja. Let's head to our offices."

In the car, Sabi continued the conversation.

"Dan tells me you were in the army with him and served in Afghanistan."

"True, I hear you also have a lot of field experience."

"I do, but as you have likely heard, mostly as a mercenary,"

"I would like to hear more about that while I am here. Obviously, I am part African and I have a deep interest in the history here in the past forty years."

"I'm happy to talk about it, but my perspective is low level. Big guys decide to become warlords, people like me do the dirty work. I will tell you more while you are here."

We arrived at the chain link gates of a large compound with a two-storey warehouse in the centre. Sabi parked and led me into the JaMAC primary warehouse and upstairs to the offices.

"I am going to set you up in James' office, Alida. I assume that you need access to his computer. My office is right here, next door to his, so if you need anything, just shout."

Sabi directed me to take the chair behind the desk and he sat across from me.

"Sabi, you told Dan that you cannot access JaMAC's bank accounts?"

"I can get at our accounts here, and cash from current sales is there, but James empties those accounts regularly. He doesn't want to attract the attention of Obissey, who is always looking for more, or from international bodies looking into the arms trade. There are several offshore accounts in the Turks and Caicos that must hold the bulk of JaMAC funds."

"And there isn't enough in the local accounts to meet our needs?"

"No, Alida, we will need about two million US for the mercenaries and another quarter of a million for arms and supplies. Dan tells me that you can get access to the JaMAC funds we need to fund this adventure."

"He should have said that I MAY be able to get into the bank accounts. There are no guarantees and no promises on how long it might take if I can do it. It really depends on how securely everything was set up by James."

"Sabi, if I figure out how to access the offshore funds, how will we pay the mercs?"

"I could use your help with details on this, Alida. We have been supplying arms, and even personnel, to some of the bigger mining companies in Africa for mine security protection, so we have contacts with them. I have created dummy mining companies in several smaller African banks, and we can use those to pay the mercenaries as mine security staff. We already have JaMAC accounts in several nearby countries, to accept payments from the mining companies."

"Why not just use those accounts and pay out 'mine security' directly from there?

"I thought it may look more legitimate, and more confusing, if JaMAC transferred funds to the fake mining companies and then paid the staff from there."

"Good idea, Sabi. Any issues setting up these fake accounts?"

"Some of these banks are dodgy and, in any case, the names of the companies read like they are real companies, and a little bribery can help. We only really need one account to pay the mercs, although two might be better, just to further muddy the waters."

"Sabi, can you access James' computer?"

"Sure, I know his password."

"Okay, leave me to it. It may take a day or two, but I'm going to try hard to get into those other accounts."

I started at the most basic level, looking for files that might contain bank information and passwords. There were a lot of files, mostly unencrypted Word, Excel, PDF, PowerPoint. There was some video as well. I opened each one, looking to see if the titles might be a giveaway and that the information might be hiding in plain sight. No such luck.

Next, I started looking through emails for potential bank correspondence. I was able to determine that there were emails with the American-Caribbean Bank in the Turks and Caicos, but the correspondence dealt with investment transactions and nothing about account numbers.

There was a lot of correspondence dealing with JaMAC's business. Although the language was somewhat coded, the emails dealt with the potential sourcing of goods in Georgia, Armenia, and Belarus, so highly likely about arms. Some were emails back and forth dealing with payments, deliveries, and shipments.

The recycle bin had more than six thousand files in it. I needed to include these in my search in case James thought that simply deleting a file meant that it would be permanently gone. That seemed unlikely because there were quite a few encrypted files on his machine as well. A sign that he was somewhat security aware.

Anyway, this was my thing. I didn't mind spending time wading through files and could work quickly on the unencrypted files, searching for anything useful for banking.

In the MS-Outlook deleted files folder, I found emails dealing with another company named JaPERS mixed in with the JaMAC business correspondence. These also appeared to be owned by James. On the surface, JaPERS looked like some sort of staffing or personnel company that was locating people in Doadja for placement in job openings in Europe. But when I read through these, I noticed something very disturbing under the surface. Although the language was mostly couched in business terms, there were some in which things seemed to go wrong, and James or parties at the other end were expressing concern or even fear. By looking at the email addresses and doing some digging on the Web, I started to realize that James was running an operation moving young women from Doadja and other African countries to Europe. On the surface, they were being placed in household domestic positions or health care services, but the organizations that James was dealing with didn't appear to be in that line of work. It was clear to me, after not too much digging, that James was running an operation that was trafficking sex-workers into Europe. One email in particular was a key giveaway:

James, keep it coming. Our clients like them young – for fourteen to sixteen they will pay a premium.

Nobody wants a fourteen-year-old personal support worker. Jesus, this old friend of Dad's is looking like one of the overall worst people in the world. The arms trade is bad enough, but human trafficking, including children! That's beyond the pale!

I walked out of the office and down to Sabi's office.

"Sabi, tell me about JaPERS."

"Alida, I don't know much about that."

"Get serious, you are moving people from here to Europe and you don't know much about it?"

"Honestly, I tried not to be involved at all. I just wanted to focus on JaMAC."

"But you do know what that business is, right?"

"You mean emigration assistance?"

"No, I mean sex-trade human trafficking?"

"Oh, that."

"Yes, that. How long has that been going on? "

"The past three years."

"Why, isn't there enough money in arms?"

"No, it's not about that. You know that the arms trade from the old soviet countries involves organized crime and some very nasty characters. James was pressured into it by one of these groups. It was one of the crime groups that presented as a package deal – add the movement of people from Doadja and surrounding countries or we will cut off the arms trade and drive you out of business. There may have even been threats to his personal safety."

"God, I don't really care about the reason, this is really disgusting. Was it big money as well?"

"Yes, JaPERS pays a small amount to families here, lies about the future for their young women, and then gets major payments from organized crime groups in Europe."

"A related question. Was this revenue shared with Obissey?"

"I don't know, Alida. As I said, I tried to keep my nose out of it."

"If it wasn't, would Obissey be pissed? Could this be why he locked up James?"

"It's possible, Alida. Maybe his approach is that everything is his, including any side-businesses that James may have started."

I turned and walked out of Sabi's office. Jesus, I needed some time on my own. I sat in James' office just staring at the wall. What a can of worms. Until this trafficking issue came to light, I was enjoying this adventure of getting James free. Now, it makes me kind of sick.

Once I was able to re-focus, I turned my attention to the banking transactions. The local bank accounts were unencrypted and it was easy to identify the payments to Obissey's personal accounts in Switzerland, because they were the only substantial transfers to a Swiss account. Other transfers appeared to go to offshore banks elsewhere. Looking at the revenue streams, and the fact that there were no local accounts related to JaPERS, tended to confirm that all funds going to Obissey were related to JaMAC business.

I went back to Sabi's office.

"Sabi, it looks to me like nothing related to JaPERS accounts is here and that any profit-sharing with Obissey was limited to JaMAC. If the President became aware of the human trafficking operation, it wouldn't take long for him to figure out that James had not included any revenues from that in his calculations of what was owed to him."

"Hmm, then it is quite possible that he could have found out about the trafficking. The public cover story of finding employment in Europe for young women is well known in the community."

"Well, Sabi, I think we now know the reason why Obissey grabbed James. There is a certain rough justice to it, but the death sentence that Wailing Island represents is a bit harsh."

I turned and went back to James' office. I was fuming. *What had we got ourselves into, trying to get this pond scum out?* I made myself some instant coffee in the nearby kitchen and tried to calm down.

It was time to get at the encrypted files, and there remained two of those to deal with. I had access to some great tools from my office, including Passware Kit Ultimate, Elcomsoft Forensic, and Hashcat. If someone at KPMG office noticed I was using these outside my work environment, it could be a problem, but it's not likely, and I would deal with that when it happened.

Within an hour I had decrypted one of the encrypted files. It was a list of four long numbers, each item a complex mix of numbers and letters. These looked like the passwords for four different bank accounts, but without account numbers. I was hoping that the second file might include the bank info and account numbers, but it dealt entirely with JaPERS. It was contact information for individuals in Amsterdam and Belgrade, along with some notes for numbers of shipments, dates, and payment requirements. Not what I was looking for.

So, without knowing the bank and account details for the accounts, I still didn't have access to them. Time to go back through all the unencrypted files to see if this info was buried there. I started with Word files, opening each file, and browsing through every page of text. Same with the PDFs. Next, the Excel files, again, looking at every page to see if James had hidden the information on unlabelled second or third pages. Then the PowerPoints, looking at every slide. Nothing.

Then I remembered something that I had seen elsewhere, the hiding of text behind images in PowerPoint. I went into PowerPoint again, except this time I moved every image, to see if James had hidden anything behind them. Then bingo! In a file that was labelled "Mustique House" that was filled with photos of a beautiful house that I assume was on Mustique. I moved an image on page nine, which revealed what were clearly, by their structure and spacing, bank routing and account numbers. When I looked up the routing information, it indicated that it was indeed for the American-Caribbean Bank in the Turks and Caicos.

Now I had to find a way to match up the accounts and passwords. The most logical thing, given that James thought that they were well-hidden or encrypted, would be that the accounts and passwords would be in the same order of one to four.

I went back to see Sabi.

"Sabi, I have the accounts. Give me the routing and account info for the bogus mine accounts and I will make some smallish transfers to see if it works."

It did work! I transferred one hundred thousand dollars from each of the four accounts. Two into one of the bogus mine accounts and two into the other accounts. We were in business.

There was more than enough in the Turks accounts. In fact, we could withdraw all that we needed for the coup from any one of the four accounts. Overall, there must have been a hundred and forty million USD in those accounts.

I wrote down some instructions, along with account and password info for Sabi, instructing him to start transferring random-sized amounts daily to the bogus mining company accounts we had set up. Transactions were not to be larger than one hundred thousand dollars and should include some small transfers until the amounts we needed were in the fake mining company accounts.

"Sabi, I am done here until the coup. I have booked my flight out tomorrow. On this paper is the info that you need to get the required amounts into the right accounts, whenever needed. I will be back for the coup."

"Okay, Alida. What does Dan have in mind for you during the coup?"

"I am going to use the fact that I am a Black woman to blindside the air force and tower people at the airport. The idea is to enable me to walk right in and catch them off-guard."

Sabi smiled,

"You are probably right; they won't be expecting a woman to show up."

"Not just a woman, I am dressing to the max and will be loaded with gold jewellery, so that the initial reaction will be that I must be part of the President's following. They will hesitate to take any action at all."

"Sounds like a plan. Nice working with you. I will see you when you are back here."

Back at the hotel, I laid on the bed and thought about the JaPERS situation. *Should I tell the team about this?* I don't know if it was the right answer, but I decided not to. I know Dad would be incredulous. Clearly, he and Matt thought that James was an adventurer, but not an amoral criminal. Better to leave that aside for now, at least until this operation is over. When I rebooked the flight home, I built in a stopover in Amsterdam. I had some business to attend to there on my way home.

135

for now, at least until this operation is over. When I rebooked the flight home, I built in a stopover in Amsterdam. I had some business to attend to there on my way home.

Chapter 14.
Nadeem - May

With the coup plan sufficiently detailed, Nadeem logged into Civ VI. Once in, he set up a game, selected his character, and sent the game invitation to Lare and Sabi. As scheduled, they were both already logged into Civ and responded to the invitation. He waited for them to join the game he had started and then initiated play. For about fifteen minutes he played what seemed like a normal game, and then he went to the chat function and sent a message to Lare.

It would be great to see you again. I will be in Amsterdam next week, any chance we could get together?

I already have a visa but will be in Munich for an economics conference. Would that work?

Sure, where will you be staying?

The Sofitel Bayerpost, adjacent to the Hauptbahnhof.

Okay, I know it. I will book there. When will you not be in the conference?

Tuesday afternoon, and evenings are free.

Okay, see you in the Sofitel lobby at 13:00 Tuesday.

He made a few Civ moves and continued with the game for another ten minutes, and then indicated to the others that he was logging off. Sunday night he flew to Munich via Toronto.

At one p.m. Tuesday, he was sitting in the dramatic, blue-lit lobby of the Sofitel, when he saw Lare coming from the elevator lobby area.

"Rafael, good to see you again."

"And you, my friend."

"It is a lovely day; I suggest we walk and chat."

Out on Bayerstrasse, Nadeem started:

"It seems more secure to be out of the hotel, I assume that Obissey at least keeps some kind of eye on you."

"I agree."

"I have a much more developed plan to present to you. My purpose today is to demonstrate to you that we have a workable plan, and to show you how we have attempted to minimize the risk to you, both now, and as the coup unfolds."

"Great, I look forward to hearing it."

"I will talk as we walk, Rafael, but at some point, we will need to find a corner in a coffee shop, where I can show you some details. Do you know Munich?"

"No, it's my first time here."

"There is a great pedestrian area nearby where we can walk and talk without worrying about traffic or traffic noise. Let's wait until we are in that area for me to tell you more."

Nadeem guided Rafael up Bayerstrasse the one block to the pedestrian tunnel to Karlsplatz.

"From here, there is a long stretch of pedestrian-only streets as far as Marienplatz. Have you done any more thinking, Rafael, about your willingness to take this risk?"

"No major shift. If the plan is feasible, I am willing to risk it all, for my family and for the country."

"Good, let me give you the general picture. We have a special forces officer on our team. He went to Doadja, scouted out the critical locations, like the palace, the prison, the Guard barracks, and other key points before he developed the plan. He also tried to get a feel for the general situation, and that led into the plan. Overall, his plan is to use the element of surprise and act stunningly quickly, so that the coup will be over in less than an hour. The idea is to undermine any residual loyalty to Obissey by indicating that the change is a done deal before any opposition can really mobilize."

"We will block access from the army barracks on the island, breach the palace, and eliminate Obissey. We will also seize the airport, to eliminate a response from the air force, and stop any attempt of the off-duty palace guard to enter the city. This will all happen within an elapsed time of one hour maximum, with most of the activity occurring within a much shorter window."

"When you say eliminate, do you mean kill? I am not comfortable with Obissey being killed. Are there alternatives?"

"Rafael, you need to come to grips with that. It is an essential item. If he is alive, there is an excuse for some residual fighting. We need to discourage the Guard from taking any follow-up action and we want the people to be publicly celebrating as quickly as possible. Also, if Obissey is dead, Doadja has a real possibility of recovering the funds that Obissey has stashed in offshore accounts: alive, he can contest that at every step."

"Our plan has you arriving in the country at the same time as the coup is underway. As soon as we seize the comms centre, we will load a taped video and audio message from you, and then within twenty minutes of the coup kick-off, we will have you doing live interviews from the comm centre. The public must know as soon as possible that Obissey is gone and that you are the new President. This will also be your opportunity to present your policies and to reassure the country that there will be a substantial change in the near future."

"Please keep exploring other options. I really dislike the idea of starting my government with murders."

"Fine, Rafael, but I believe the death of Obissey and his wife if she is in-country will be the only way to protect your future. If you can, try to think in terms of the dozens of Doadjans who 'disappeared' during his reign."

"What about other fatalities, Nadeem?"

"We anticipate heavy fatalities among the Presidential Guard. In fact, all at the palace will be eliminated, and most of the off-duty Guard, except those who surrender. Other than that, there will only be a few more fatalities – the head of the army and the Guard, possibly a couple at the airport, and some at the entrance to the island base as we discourage them from attempting to cross the bridge."

"Who are our forces, Nadeem, and how will they get into the country?"

"They are mercenaries, some Doadjan, many not. They will be coming into the country in the days and hours beforehand. Some will travel on foot through the national park, while others will be hidden in shipments destined for the palace."

"What if Obissey is not in the palace?"

"Of course, we will need to know if he is up-country or out of the country. If we confirm he is at home, we plan to attack the palace at seven in the evening. Our information is that he is always at dinner in the palace dining room at that time. We like that time also because the roads will also be busy with end-of-day traffic, which will help impede movement by the Guard."

By this time, they were approaching the *Café Guglhopf.*

"Let's go in here, Rafael, and find a table where I can show you the details."

They worked their way to the back and found a table away from other customers.

"I'm having a coffee, Rafael. For you?"

"Same please, with milk."

When the server came, Nadeem ordered in his best tourist German.

"Zwei café bitte, eine swartz, eine mit milch."

Once the coffee arrived, Nadeem pulled a folded stack of papers from his jacket pocket and handed them to Rafael. Rafael studied them while Nadeem drank his coffee and casually looked around to see if anyone was making a point of watching them. There didn't appear to be, and there was a brisk turnover in coffee shop customers as Rafael read.

"Nadeem, you are planning to take over an entire country with about fifty people. Very daring."

"Who dares wins, Rafael. Seriously, though, it depends on a couple of key things. First, the army must really be ambivalent or negative about Obissey. If the regiment on the island continues to fight their way into the city, eventually they will succeed because of their numbers. If the two regiments in the country decide to mobilize and come into Nambi, the coup will fail for sure."

"You know, Nadeem, I have lived outside the country for some years, but what I have heard from family and friends in Doadja is that the army will not fight if they are given an opportunity to avoid it. Not only do they not support Obissey, but they are poorly led. The general leading the army is an Obissey cousin and that is his sole credential. They are also poorly equipped. Obissey put his trust in the Presidential Guard and didn't want the army to get too powerful."

"What do you feel are the critical points, Nadeem?"

"Rafael, the other key factors will be our ability to penetrate the palace and eliminate Obissey, and our success in seizing the communications centre. Of course, all the elements of the plan must work, but those two, and the army passivity, are key. I know the plan to simply block the army on the island seems daring and simplistic, but we only need to contain them for less than an hour. If your reading is right about the weak loyalty to the President, that should work."

"Tell me about go/no-go decision points."

"The first will be soon. We need to know we can line up the mercenaries and can get them into adjacent countries posing as mine security personnel. If we can't do that, we can't proceed."

"The next critical point will be just prior to the Canadians leaving for Doadja. We will need a final check to ensure that everything is in place. That will be four days before the coup. At that point, the day will be set and the jet arranged to pick you up on the day of the coup."

"The last checkpoint will be just before your flight enters Doadjan airspace. If somehow the government has detected or engaged one of the border crossings, or Obissey suddenly leaves town, or there is any evidence of mobilization of the Guard or army, we will shut it down immediately."

"Let me settle up for the coffees on the way out and meet you out front. Let's keep walking."

Rafael was in the pedestrian mall, looking in shop windows when Nadeem emerged.

"Let's continue down Kaufingerstrasse here, it will take us to Marianplatz, really the heart of the city."

"Rafael, do you have other concerns that we can address?"

"Just one," Lare smiled.

"Naturally, I have a general concern for my life and the lives of my parents and children of course, but that kind of fear is what has kept Obissey in power. There is a continuous level of fear among the entire population. If we are ever to have a better country, someone needs to take the leap. Someone who dares, as you say."

"Rafael, it will still take time to get everything in place. If you think of other specifics we need to address, you can contact us. That brings me to security. Can you get disposable burner phones in Senegal?"

"Ha, every phone is a burner phone in Senegal. They are ridiculously cheap there."

"Then get a burner and load it with the Signal app. When everyone is equipped that way, we will drop the Civilization route for communicating. Even when we are using encrypted messaging, avoid any words that might cause a computer analysis of messages to raise a flag – Doadja, coup, mercenaries, Canadians, for example. I would like the documents with the timing and resources back. It is safer if you don't travel back to Africa with those in hand."

"Are you good to keep walking?"

Lare indicated he was enjoying the walk, so the two of them headed into the market area and wandered for another hour, while discussing some coup details.

"Rafael, there is an issue that we need to discuss. We will line up the funds to make the initial payment of fifty percent to the mercenaries, but your government will have to be able to pay the balance and pay it quickly."

"Understood, how much is involved?"

"The estimate is that you will need to be able to pay about two million dollars. Payment will be made to one of the pseudo mine companies that we have set up, and the mercenaries will be paid from that account. Their payments will appear to come from a mining company for security services rendered."

"Please understand that the group members from Canada are not doing this for money. We have already arranged for JaMAC to pay our travel expenses. No government funds will be paid to the Canadians. This is important to us. If it ever somehow comes out that we had some involvement, we want it to be clear that this wasn't some kind of get rich scheme. There have been too many of those in Africa."

Nadeem then suggested that they head back.

"Rafael, how do you feel about beer and German food?"

"Well, not on the top of my list, but since we are here, why not? Do you know a good spot?"

"I do know an excellent, very traditional place on the pedestrian route back, the Augustiner Stammhaus. It's a landmark in Munich."

It took a good half-hour to get back to the Augustiner.

"There are more formal dining areas upstairs, Rafael, but I suggest we go full Bavarian and eat here in the bierhall."

"Great, I love the old, panelled walls."

After a few minutes reading the menu, Rafael chuckled:

"I don't know German food, but the English menu includes Corrugated Meat and Slaughter Bowl. I am assuming that is an issue with translation, rather than an accurate description."

"Exactly, the slaughter bowl is a plate of assorted sausages made with blood, like boudin, and the corrugated meat is a pork belly dish. These do remind me of another dish that made me smile. In Bulawayo, I had roast baby beef buttock. Perhaps an accurate description, but one of which I would rather not know the details.”

Lare ordered venison goulash, and Nadeem had roasted duck. Afterwards, they talked briefly on the street.

“Rafael, I appreciate that you are willing to go forward and your motives are good. When we complete the coup, I hope that you can stay true to your intentions and not evolve to become another ‘big man’ ruler.”

Lare responded,

“Given Africa’s history, I understand your concern. Any promises I might make to you at this point would be meaningless. You and I will just have to hope for the best.”

“Rafael, you need to be thinking about the transition. Specifically, the taped message, your initial address, and your response to media questions at the comms centre. But also, how you will run the government, and who you can trust to act in your cabinet and to lead the army. Also, what will you do about the remainder of the palace Guard? All in all, you have a lot of thinking to do, Rafael.”

“Nadeem, do you think I will have support from outside the country once I take over?”

“The Western developed countries will come on side quickly if they see your intent is to create a better environment for your people. You will need to be initially careful in dealing with the oil companies, so that they don’t try to move against you. Some of the African countries like Zimbabwe and Congo will initially oppose you, at least in a symbolic way, because many of them are frightened of coups against their own terrible governments. But they are unlikely to take any action against you or Doadja and will come on side at some point.”

“Will we meet again?”

“Nothing personal, but I hope not anytime soon. The less we meet the better. We will do our best not to let you down. Perhaps you can invite me as an official guest once things settle down after the coup.”

“Of course, goodbye, Nadeem, and thanks.”

Chapter 15.
Sabi - May

Job One was to get floor plans, or at least a reasonably reliable sketch of the layout of the palace. We needed to break through in an area that was near the dining room and which would allow us to move quickly into other areas.

The trick was how to get this information without raising suspicion. That ruled out existing palace staff and ex-staff that were from Obissey's tribe. I needed someone who had worked there for some years but was retired and had no blood connection to Obissey. If they had left the capital and gone back to their own village, so much the better. Family networks seemed the best for a "no questions asked" approach.

I drove out to my family's hometown. My parents were dead, but I still had relatives there, including aunt Einid. I hadn't been back there for years. I needed to spend some time and be social before gently asking.

The drive out was on a typical Doadjan road. The government had paved it back in colonial days, but not since, so it was a grinding journey with huge potholes. In some areas where there wasn't forest, the road was three or four lanes wide because people had tried to drive around potholes, then drive around the new potholes.

Of course, even on the relatively short drive to the village I ran into one of the Presidential Guard's informal, random checkpoints. These were more about a shakedown than any real security issue. Two armed guards had dragged a sawhorse type barrier across the road. They were typical Presidential Guard thugs. The fat one, with his AK slung across his belly, waddled up to the door of the car. The muzzle of his rifle was resting on the windowsill. Given how hopeless these clowns are, the weapon was probably too dirty to fire, but I wasn't about to test it.

"Where you go?"

"Visiting hometown."

"Let me see your papers – driver's license, vehicle ownership."

I was ready for this and had them laying on the passenger seat, with the equivalent of about five dollars in local currency stuck between the pages. The guards took the pages, pretended to read them (many of these guys are completely uneducated), and then handed them back, minus the cash.

"Okay, then, you can go."

"Thank you."

It took me two and half hours to get there, but it hadn't changed much so it was easy to find Einid's modest home. It was a simple one room dwelling with a kind of kitchen set up outside behind the house. I knocked on the door and called out:

"Einid, it's your nephew Sabi."

I could hear the shuffle of feet, and then Einid came to the door. Like many of the people in Doadja, Einid looked older than her years. I remember her as being young when I was a child. I think she is maybe eight or ten years older than me, but she looks ninety. Hard field work and a poor diet of mostly cassava and maize have left her tiny, wizened, and bent over. But she still greeted me with a warm smile.

"Sabi, oh my, it has been so very long. Look at you."

"Yes, Einid, sorry it has been years, I was away from Doadja for many years."

"And now?"

"I am living in Nambi, Auntie."

"And what do you do there, Sabi? Nothing good seems to happen there."

"A variety of things, I am eating. Enough about me, are you well?"

"Look at me, Sabi, I am old. Of course, I am not well, but I am as good as can be expected. Come, help me bring chairs out here in the sun, I will make tea."

I carried out two old plastic chairs to the dirt in front of the house, while Enid shuffled around inside. After a while, she came out with two mugs, one tin, one ceramic. She served me a strong brewed tea with milk.

"What brings you back to us, Sabi?"

"I need some help from family, or maybe a close friend here."

"How can we help?"

"I have been asked to make some changes to Obissey's palace, just repairing walls and painting, but they want me to provide a price and I don't know the layout at all – how many rooms, how they fit together. That sort of thing."

"We hear in the village that it is all foreigners from Italy and France that do the work on the palace. That money doesn't matter at all."

"That may be true, but this is a small-small job, so they asked me."

"How do they know you? You are not close to that gang of thieves, are you?"

"No, Auntie, it is just that I am known in Nambi for undertaking construction and repair work."

"I still do not understand how I can help."

"I am hoping that here in the village, there may be someone that worked in the palace for years, then retired, that could draw me a sketch of what it is like inside. I have never been there."

This wasn't entirely true. I had been there many times with James, but only to the front public offices area to meet with Obissey.

"I am thinking, Sabi. Maybe Adama down the road. I will go and ask."

Einid headed out at a slow walk and I sat back, waiting. It may have been half an hour.

"She did work in the palace, Sabi. She only left there two years ago and when I told you why you needed it, she said she would be happy to help."

Einid then took me over to Adama's and introduced me. Although she wasn't much younger than Einid, her work at the palace had been less demanding than field work, and clearly, she had been better fed at the palace. She even looked a bit more prosperous, with a bright, Nigerian-style dress and her hair in a coloured wrap as well.

"Adama, I don't know if you remember my nephew Sabi, he came to visit me from time-to-time, years ago."

"Hello, Sabi, Einid told me about your potential work at the palace. How can I help?"

"I was wondering, Adama, if we could work together on a sketch of the palace layout? I would like to understand where the big areas are and to have an idea of the sizes."

"Well, I cannot draw very well, but I can describe things, and if you can draw it, I can tell you if it feels about right. Let me make some tea, then I will talk about the palace."

Einid and I waited patiently while the tea was prepared. On a stool, I laid greyish sheet of paper torn from a cheap school copy book, ready to draw as Adama talked. When all three of us had our cups, Adama started.

"Sabi, you have likely been in the public side of the palace. That is the side facing towards the ocean, facing West. It has all the public spaces and is about one third of the total palace. Behind that, as you move away from the ocean, there is what I call government space. This is mostly offices and meeting rooms. This is where the key civil servants like the chief of staff have offices, and where the President meets with officials. This makes up the middle of the palace, but it is not that big."

"Behind that is what I call ceremonial space. This is where all the beautifully decorated rooms are, a large reception area, a very large dining room, and the spaces that support that – the kitchens, etc."

"At the very back of the palace is the President's private, secure area. This is around a quarter of the total palace space. It includes all of the President's living quarters and can be secured separately to protect him. That area has no windows, only skylights."

I sketched in pencil as Adama talked and presented her with a first sketch.

"No, that isn't exactly right, the private area is more in the back corner on the right side. There is a corridor that runs from this area to connect to the ceremonial spaces, the government spaces, and the public spaces. It rounds across the back of the palace and then up the south side."

"Adama, is there a wall around the palace?"

"No, Sabi, the outer wall of the palace is the wall."

"How do supplies, such as food, go in, and where does garbage come out of the palace? Is there a special service entrance? You know, a kind of a side entrance with a loading dock where that kind of thing happens?"

"No, Sabi, I think for security, the only entrance to the palace is through the courtyard at the front of the palace. Everything in and out is cleared at the guardhouse. The food supplies coming in and the garbage handling are all done through there at night so as not to be visible to visitors to the palace."

I revised the sketch and presented it to her again.

"Yes, that is it. I never paid attention to the sizes of things, but the locations are right and I think the proportions are okay as well."

"Thank you, Adama, this gives me what I need to make a good proposal."

"You are welcome, Sabi. I wish you luck. Please tell Einid if you succeed in getting the job. I would like to know."

It was a rough, hand-drawn sketch, but according to Einid it captured the general layout, which is what we needed:

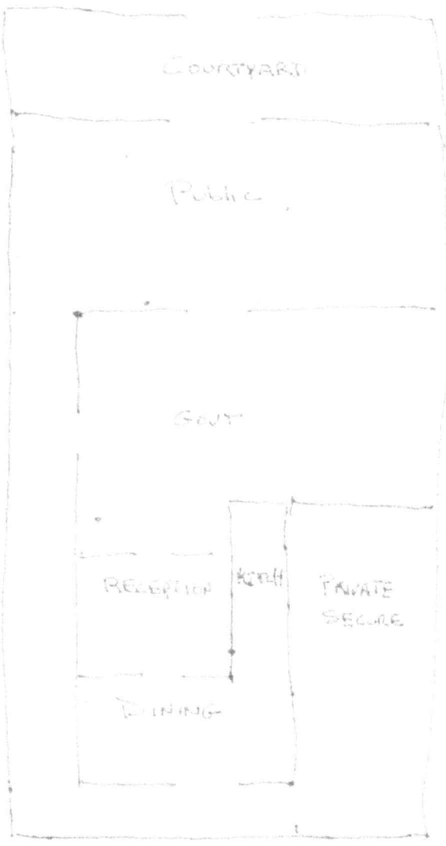

The next day, I took a picture of the sketch, drove over the border out of Doadja, and emailed the sketch to Dan, with a note:

Our holiday pics turned out as expected, enjoy.

It was time to set the old merc network in motion. While I was out of Doadja and using a new burner phone, I started my calls. I knew I would only need to call four or five of the more senior guys and it could fan out from there. I called five. Three were currently active in Congo, so clearly up for the job. These were five guys I had trusted with my life; Olivier, Kurt, Adan, Bami, and Chris. They would make excellent team leaders if they were in. I started with Olivier. He was the closest friend in that group, we had been through a lot together. English was the common language among this diverse group.

"Hello."

"Olivier, it's Sabi. Where have I found you?"

"Sabi, old friend. I am still in Congo, up-country doing mine security work. Horrible place here."

"I knew you would be someplace horrible, it's what you do."

"Too true, my friend. Where are you?"

"Home here in Doadja. You must remember I changed jobs and started working with James MacKenzie. I'm still doing that."

"Yes of course, why do you call? A sales call?"

"No, no sales. I have a potential short-term job for you and some of our old friends. Two weeks, some of the same old gang doing the same old thing. High pay, for you twenty thousand before and twenty thousand after, and for team members, fifteen and fifteen."

"Are we talking American dollars here? And the usual second payment on completion, to the worker or to the family if he cannot collect?"

"Yes. I will also need some special skills, including a couple of engineers, and a couple of air traffic controllers. Higher rates are negotiable for those. The others can be our usual players, but they need experience. The job will be fast, but maybe intense."

"How many do you need altogether?"

"About fifty in total. I am going to call four others that you know as possible team leaders, so be thinking of ten to twenty from your end."

"When do you need to know, and when is the job likely to happen?"

"I will call you in four days and the job will be sometime in the next two months."

"Sabi, a lot of the guys know you. If I mention your name, they will most likely be in."

"You can mention my name. By the way, don't contact anyone currently working for Wagner. I don't want leakage of any activity going back to the Russian government. Who knows where that would lead. Once we know who the team is, I will be sending out employment letters from mines to help the members get into place for the job."

"How much lead time will we have?"

"At least two weeks, and maybe a bit longer."

"Sounds good, Sabi. Many of your old companions are here in Congo along with many younger workers with the skills you need. I won't have much trouble getting hold of them."

"Great. Talk to you in four days, Olivier."

I repeated this call with the other four, covering the same ground of time, pay, special requirements, etc. and arranged to call each of them back in four days. I would need to go out of Doadja again to make those calls.

My next priority was to check for weapons, etc. Much of it we already had in inventory at JaMAC, ready to ship to customers. All the assault rifles, heavy machine guns, sniper rifles, suppressors and RPGs were already in hand. We had a shipment of C4 that was enroute to Equatorial Guinea and I could divert that to our warehouse here. The shaped charges for the palace wall were the biggest challenge. We could work around that by building our own. With copper plates and the C4, we could build those in two days.

Vehicles were really no problem; we had our own trucks and army trucks I can get for short-term use through bribery. We would use our own truck for the palace breach, so that we could modify the rear-end and add the explosives. We would also need to modify the sides, because we needed to be able to offload everyone in seconds before the demolition, so they would be ready to rush into the breach.

For the bridge, army trucks will work well. The sentries at the base entrance might wonder why they are backing onto the bridge but would see that they were army and ignore them for key seconds.

Two more trucks to create a complete traffic block on the highway into the city from the Guard base were no problem. They could be ours as well. Cars were no problem. If necessary, we will just steal some that day.

A few days later I was back out of Doadja again to make the follow-up calls. Luckily, our business had taken me in and out so often, the border guards simply waved. Our deliveries of scotch from time to time helped as well.

I booked into a local hotel in a nearby small town and got on the phone.

"Olivier, it's Sabi. How is it going?"

"Great, Sabi. For you, almost everybody I get in touch with is interested in your 'mining security' assignment. The pay seems reasonable and they can be ready to roll on a few days' notice. I have fifteen interested, with the kind of skills that you requested."

"Great. I will need names and emails so that I can get out the hiring letters and ID cards from our mines, and so that I can follow up with them directly when the timing is clear. Let each one of them know that the mines require secure communications and make sure that they have the Signal app active on their phones. Assemble the list, but don't send it to me until I contact you again. Talk soon, bye, Olivier."

I wanted to be outside Doadja with another new burner when the lists came in.

I repeated similar calls with Kurt, Adan, Bami, and Chris. Overall, we had about fifty-five candidates. A few may drop out (or be killed in their current jobs) before our mission. The number was good.

When I got back to Nambi, I went on Civ VI that evening, and once the game was going, I entered a short message in the chat function.

All good here, effective team is building. Let's set a date when we can get together. I will need three weeks to make travel arrangements at my end. It is time to move to Signal and wrap up this game. We will communicate through Signal from here on.

Dan responded.

Would love to see everyone as soon as possible. I propose Canada Day, 1 July. We can celebrate together. We will need to finalize by 26 June. Important that our key target is home on 1 July. Sabi, can you verify?

Two days later I headed back out of Doadja, got a new burner, and settled into a little hotel. I called each of my team leaders, had them send me the contact info as jpg attachments titled "mine security." I worked my way down the lists, emailing each merc in Signal with tailored information – date to enter adjacent country. I wanted to move people into two RV points over a two-week period. A bunch of hard looking men showing up all at once at airports or border crossings might attract too much interest. A few mine security guys showing up each day, hopefully not as much.

In our own warehouse in Nambi, I had the crew set up an enclosed living space on the mezzanine floor in the back. The three Canadians and the mercs would need to bunk and eat there for two days before the coup. We needed everyone in place two days early for preparation. The coup timing was critical, so we couldn't be fumbling around.

Finally, I sent a Signal message back to all.

The First of July is a great day to get together here, everyone, including the prominent people we need to meet, will be in the city that day. There have already been events announced that will involve the top people.

Chapter 16.
Sabi - June

By early June, we were in motion. I set up two RV points, both remote. There is an abandoned sugar mill not too far from the border, and near Doadja National Park, on this side of the border. The other is a warehouse in the same area only twenty kilometres from the Doadja border, and not far off the main road leading to Doadja. It was empty, and I was able to rent it for two months for a nominal sum. I directed our staff to start stocking these facilities with food and bedding. For sure, this would generate questions, but most JaMAC people are ex-mercs in any case, and paid well to mind their own business and to keep quiet. We didn't expect authorities to stumble upon these two sites, but local farmers might get inquisitive. I arranged for our guards, dressed in security firm outfits, to keep people out.

The team leaders will be at the RV points first, to manage and contain the "boys." I also need these leaders in place early because I want them to take the palace team through rehearsal drills. I made sure that I directed the people that I wanted on the palace team, to the warehouse location. There was room there to set up a mock-up.

27 June

By the twenty-seventh of June, the palace team was supposed to be in place at the RV outside Doadja, so I headed back out of Doadja and made my way to the rented warehouse, taking lots of precautions and roundabout routes.

When I got there, everyone was assembled and ready to go. It was exciting to be back with an action team. I had fought beside some of the more senior guys in various places. Even several of the younger troops knew me from deliveries that JaMAC had made.

Using the various cardboard boxes that the food and bedding had come in, I had the palace team set up a mock-up of the palace layout on the floor of the warehouse. Once that was done, I launched into my detailed briefing.

"Guys, here's the deal. We are going to overthrow the government in Doadja. You may know that the prick in charge and his dad have been running the country into the ground for many years. There have been no attempts to take him out, the whole place is complacent and the army is ambivalent. The key enemy is Obissey's own Palace Guard. They not only guard the palace but they also function as his personal gestapo to keep the population in line.

"The key to this coup is speed – we will be taking out all key functions at once. The mission of this team, the palace team, is to breach the palace, take out Obissey, and eliminate the Guard troops at the palace. I want this whole operation done in less than ten minutes. I will walk you through the steps. First, a small group of four will set up a frontal attack on the palace – mostly staying in cover, using maximum firepower for noise and distraction, and taking out the guards at the palace entrance. This should also draw guards from inside the palace. At the same time, the main part of the force will arrive at the east wall of the palace in a specially prepared stake truck. It has been modified to enable offloading directly from the bed of the truck on both sides to enable everyone to offload simultaneously. The truck will be backed up against the palace wall. As soon as you are offloaded, take a prone position because we are going to blow the wall inward, and there may be backscatter."

With that, I walked them through the mock-up. I used a stick as a pointer as I talked.

"As soon as the wall is breached, I need two of you," and I pointed to two of the guys, "you and you, to break right and immediately enter and seal off the private quarters. Obissey is paranoid, and this is his giant panic room, with a heavy steel door.

There will be no one in there at that time. He locks himself and his wife in there every night, but not until later. We cannot let him get into that area or we are screwed. So, get into the private quarters, close up, and open only for me or someone else from the group that you recognize. CCTV monitors will let you check who is at the door."

"The rest of the group will quickly move left, down the corridor. The first doors on the right will be the entrance to the dining room, where we expect Obissey to be at dinner time. I will lead the first four of you into the dining room, and we will take out everyone there. The rest of you will continue down the corridor and into the public areas taking out the guards as you go. Continue until you have reached the palace courtyard entrance and the guards are all down or have surrendered. Once the dining room is clear, the dining room group will continue west toward the palace front. Be careful not to fire on our own team when we meet up heading toward the front of the palace. When we meet up with the frontal assault team, we will figure out what to do with any prisoners. Any questions?"

"How many guards?"

"There are typically twenty guards on duty at the palace. Sometimes as many as thirty."

"Any good?"

"No, these are not soldiers, they are best at abusing civilians. None of them will have ever been in a firefight. I expect panic and chaos, some hiding, just general loser stuff. I don't care if you take them all out. These are a bad bunch."

"How are we getting to the site?"

"Olivier has already been briefed, but on the day of the mission, you will be picked up here in two trucks. They will be apparently filled with alcohol in boxes, but there will be a central corridor leading to a crammed space in the front of the compartment in each truck big enough for ten or twelve standing men. There will be ceiling straps to hang on to. That's where you guys will hide. Boxes will be filled into the corridor behind you once you are loaded and in position. As the truck approaches the border, the driver will warn you, and absolute silence will be essential until you are clear of the border. These trucks will take you to our warehouse in Nambi, where you will weapon-up and load into the attack truck."

"Weapons?"

"All Eastern-Bloc stuff. You will all have AKs, and as much ammo and grenades as you can carry. Tactical vests are there for each of you as well."

"What is the end game? When do we go home?"

"The plan assumes that, with Obissey down, and the Guard taken out, the army will quickly come on side. In that case, you will all be backhauled out within four days."

"And failure?"

"You all know that failure is always possible; but if we fail to take out Obissey, or the army backs him, we will extract you by truck through the border points. In that case, we will be trying to silence the national comms to make sure that the border points are not aware. You will be armed as well, and in the same trucks that the border agents are used to seeing, so getting back across the border should be okay. You will then come back here from outside Doadja, dump the weapons, go civilian, and disperse. Other questions?"

With no more questions, I left the group and spoke to Olivier.

"Any issues with the troops?"

"No, we have been able to keep as quiet as possible and to keep everyone on site. The sentries haven't reported anyone coming by. We are still pretty much invisible."

"Good, I am heading back to Nambi. Keep a lid on it here. Expect the 'go' in the next few days."

At our end, I had the JaMAC team unpacking and cleaning weapons.

June twenty-eighth seemed to rush up. There was no indication that Obissey was out of the country or even out of Nambi. Through Signal, I let the gang know:

Good to go, all ready. Key targets here.

159

Chapter 17.
28 June – 1 July

When it received the message from Sabi on Signal, the Canadian team moved into action; cryptic messages were exchanged:

Rafael, looking forward to seeing you soon. Pickup at private jet terminal 15:00 1 July.

Sabi, transportation for Rafael needed for 1 July for 15:00 pickup.

Flights to Doadja were booked for Dan, Alida and Max to arrive June twenty-eighth.

· · · · · · · · · ·

28 June

On the twenty-eighth, the mercenary team that was entering Doadja on foot across the border and through the national park, was trucked to the drop-off point in an abandoned plantation near the border with Doadja where they were briefed by their team leader:

"Guys, here's the deal. The action is in Doadja, more details will follow when we get there. Weapons and gear will be waiting for us. We will be crossing the border on foot in groups of two or three over the next three hours. You will be picked up on the Doadja side, on a bush road two klicks from the border. You can see where the bush road starts just to the north of us on the edge of the clearing. Follow it for four klicks. When you reach that mark, which should take about forty minutes, move cautiously until you see the border fence. There are normally no guards, just an occasional patrol vehicle. Follow the fence line east about five hundred meters until you see a place where elephants have trampled down the fence. Cross there, and then move west about one klick until you pick up a road. Follow that road north for two

160

klicks, where you will find a truck waiting for you. The truck will have Adoaja Farm Supplies marked on the doors. Clear?"

Nods all around, but one question.

"What if we do run into Doadja border guards or army or whatever?"

"We need to be invisible, so take it slow and dead quiet as you go. We can't afford to take out any Doadjan officials in the days prior to action. That will give the government a heads-up that something is happening. You have lots of time, be careful.

"If no more questions, Patrice, you will lead off; take two of the guys with you. I will send groups out at twenty-minute intervals and bring up the rear."

As expected, there were no border issues. One of the groups ran into illegal bushmeat hunters, but those hunters were as eager not to engage with the group as the group was not to engage with them. The two "farm supply" trucks picked up the team and shuttled it to the JaMAC warehouse. Conveniently, the warehouse enables trucks to be driven in, so there were no scenes of guys milling around outdoors. Sabi was there to meet them. Sabi used Signal to send out a message to all.

The cows have been picked up from the meadow and are safely home.

Sabi, greeted the gang;

"Guys, welcome to Doadja. Nice to see some familiar faces. You look like a team that can get things done. Upstairs you will find an area set up for everyone to sleep. Just take a cot. You will not be leaving the warehouse until three days from now. There is an eating area and a cook. We have a pool table, some gym equipment, and a couple of ping pong tables to help you pass the time. Tomorrow, I will fill you in on the mission. I will also explain why I needed you here a few days early; we have some prep to do."

"Most of you know each other from previous jobs. I have appointed Doadjans that you have teamed with before as my captains – Olivier, Adan, Patrice, and Jose. It is important that the teams we send out are led by locals, for language and appearance reasons. This needs to look as close as possible to an all-Doadjan mission."

"These captains will be coming around to check all your gear. We need to be sure nobody was stupid enough to bring their mobile phone. If you did, you are endangering all of us. Give it up and we will return it when the mission is done. You are being paid enough to buy the latest smartphone when you get back home, in any case."

· · · · · · · · · ·

29 June

Mid-morning on the twenty-ninth, two army trucks, "borrowed" by JaMAC with a suitable bribe, arrived inbound at the Doadjan border posts.

The border guards knew the drivers, knew the trucks, and knew the cargo, but had the drivers open the cargo doors in any case, to make their token inspection. As they expected, the trucks were filled with crates of wine and liquor as "gifts" to Obissey. Without a word, each of the drivers removed a case of Johnny Walker Black from the very back of the loads and handed it to the border guards with a smile. Without any other issues, the trucks were on their way and proceeded to the JaMAC warehouse. Inside each truck, in front of the reduced cargo load, there were fourteen mercenaries, standing close together and using temporary straps hanging from the ceiling to support themselves. When they arrived at the warehouse, Sabi greeted them with the same messages about sleeping, eating, and mobile phones that he had delivered the day before to the group that came through the national park.

"Does anyone still have a mobile with them? There shouldn't be any. Turn them over to me now, or you are risking your life and those of others."

Two of the mercenaries walked forward with their phones.

"Do you two have trouble following orders? You were told repeatedly not to bring them into Doadja. If this is going to be a problem, I need to cut you from the teams, terminate any bonus, and hold you here until the mission is done. Understood?"

Both muttered "yes, sir" and returned to the disapproving looks of the rest of the group.

"Everyone, we will not be here for long, we just need a couple of days to finalize and prepare. We will be breaking into different task groups tomorrow. We will fill you in on the details tomorrow. Any questions for now?"

Silence all around.

Also, that morning, Dan, Alida, and Max arrived on their flight from Dakar. They went through the usual long queue delays at Immigration, but with some additional hassles, because Dan was returning after only being away a few weeks.

"You were here only a few weeks ago, what brings you back to Doadja?"

"Business."

"Who is this business with; what kind of business?

"My business is with JaMAC and I am engaged in the trade of weapons."

"We know JaMAC, we know that business. Mostly just Africans and sometimes Russians come to see JaMAC. We never see Canadian people here for JaMAC."

"I have old family links with the company."

The agent flipped back and forth through the passport, trying to look like he was seriously studying it, then reluctantly stamped it and handed it back to Dan.

Doadja gets so few visitors, anyone coming back creates suspicion. As before, however, the statement that they were meeting with JaMAC seemed to smooth the way.

Sabi was waiting for them outside customs.

"Hello, Dan, Alida. This must be Max. I have heard a lot about you, Absolute Max."

Max smiled. "I assume mostly good?"

"Let's just say, appropriate for the task at hand. Come on, gang, I will take you to the warehouse."

Sabi drove them to the warehouse, filling them in on the way.

"I have set up a sleeping area in the warehouse and we will have food there. The first group of soldiers came in yesterday as planned. The second group is arriving in a couple of hours. When we get to the warehouse, I will introduce you to the team and then we can brief them on their tasks for today, tomorrow, and for the first of July. Should I use your real names, or cover?"

Dan responded.

"Good point, Sabi. I haven't had time to think about that. It would be better if we used cover names, in case this goes south at some point. I will be Delta, Max will be Mike, and Alida will be Alpha. We will use these as our call signs on the radio, but it will also be how I introduce you to the mercenaries."

Sabi continued.

"I have four Doadjan team captains that I trust. Olivier will be handling the bridge, Adan will take out the Guard/army leadership, Patrice will take over the tower, and Jose will lead the frontal attack on the palace. I will lead the palace breach and attack on Obissey myself. I have drawn up a list of names for each team because I know the capabilities of most of them. We have an air traffic controller to be part of the tower team and to operate the tower, and we have an experienced high-voltage electrician to be part of the comms centre team. There are three combat engineers who will work with the explosives and the IEDs. As I said, I will be leading the palace assault team."

"Good, Sabi, let's go with your choices. Glad you have Doadjans at the point. We also will need a Doadjan-speaking merc to be part of Max's team, for the road work during the day, and so that he doesn't have to deal with any prisoners. We want to keep the Canadians as invisible as possible.

"Anything we should know about weapons and supplies?"

"Nothing important, Dan, other than, as we discussed, they are all Eastern-Bloc weapons – AK's, RPGs. The only western gear are the sniper rifles, the 50 cals and the C4."

"What about the mercenaries? Is there anyone we should be concerned about?"

"There are a couple of the guys that are a little too keen on extreme action, but I have put them on the crew that is to attack the Guard convoy. I didn't think we wanted cowboys like that on any of the other teams. Otherwise, the group is solid. I know many of them and have worked with the older guys. These are all experienced warriors who will be cool under fire."

"Sounds good, so nothing we should worry about?"

"Oh, plenty to worry about, including getting killed, but all the plans are in place."

"Perfect."

At the warehouse, Sabi got all the mercenaries together.

"Guys, I want you to meet Alpha, Delta, and Mike," Sabi pointed at Alida, Dan, and Matt. You haven't worked with these three before, but all three are experienced combat veterans and are here to provide additional skills. We are working with their plan. Delta will be overall lead, coordinating teams, shifting resources, and communicating with all team captains, using satcom units that we will be distributing before action. Delta and Mike are active special forces officers. Go ahead, Delta."

"Thanks, Sabi. Look around, guys, there are less than fifty of us and we are going to establish a new government here. No doubt, you are wondering how this can work. Well, here are the key elements:

- This will be a complete surprise attack.
- We will be very well-armed, with overwhelming firepower and skills.
- We are going to hit all key points simultaneously.
- We expect only token resistance from the army. Those of you who are not Doadjan may be surprised by this, but this is a country ready for revolution.
- The Presidential Guard will put up resistance, but they are not soldiers; just a gang of thugs in uniform. They will fight because they know that to lose likely means that the citizens will kill them.
- The team captains and their roles will be:
- Alpha and Patrice will work together to disable air force action and support the taking of the control tower operation. Callsign Alpha.
- Adan will take care of the assassinations of leaders. Callsign Bravo.
- Mike's job will be to deny access to the city by off-duty members of the Presidential Guard. He will need demolition experts with him. Callsign Mike.
- Olivier and his guys will deny access to the bridge from Wailing Island. Callsign Oscar.
- Jose will lead the front diversionary attack on the palace. Callsign Juliet.
- Sabi will command the palace breach and assault. Callsign Sierra.
- I will be leading the action to seize and take over the operation of the comms centre, which will serve as overall command centre. Callsign Delta. When we are active on satcom, be sure to send all progress reports and problems to Delta on the open net to keep all teams informed."

"We have a good plan, you are all pros, and this country needs better leadership. We have no external parties involved, no

CIA, no DGSE, no financiers behind the scenes. There are no indications of leaks, nor is there any indication of outside awareness of our actions."

"Now, we have more prep work to do. Today and tomorrow, we need to arm-up, and we need to prepare the two trucks that will be used to close down the bridge and breach the palace. On the first of July, prior to the kick-off of the action, Mike will be leading a team to do road work on the road into town from the Guard barracks."

"I need all the captains to meet with me now. As soon as that is done, the captains will assemble their teams and brief them on their missions and timings. Later this afternoon, we will be assembling the prep teams and getting to work. We will get to know you all better over the next three days."

"Let me be absolutely clear. Nobody leaves the compound: nobody even leaves the warehouse unless working on something in the compound. We don't want signs of a lot of activity here. Also, Sabi has repeatedly told you about mobile phones. Please do not try to work around this constraint. It will only be a couple of days until you are done and back home."

With that, the group dispersed, leaving only the captains, who began their briefings.

· · · · · · · · · ·

30 June

The next day, Max assembled the teams he needed to rig the trucks, along with the selected drivers. Before they added any charges to the trucks, he had the drivers practice the planned maneuvers in the compound behind the warehouse. For the bridge truck drivers, he had them set up two rows of old oil barrels, with the distance measured to be the same as the estimated width of the bridge. The practice was for the two trucks to drive past the end of the rows, then reverse and back up between the rows so that the two trucks were tight side by side. The first few times it was less than perfect, with oil barrels rolling across the pavement, but after several hours of practice it started to become a smooth operation. Those two trucks were then rigged with charges to blow off the back wheels and axles. The electric detonators were wired to the driver's position in each truck. As a last step, the windshields were removed. With Sabi's help, Max briefed the drivers.

"Guys, you won't be driving fast in town. Wind won't be a problem. We have taken the windshields out so you can bail out over the hood of the trucks once they are in place. There will not be room to open the doors because the bridge is so narrow, and by exiting over the hood, the truck will protect you if anyone decides to open fire. I will have a flashlight with a green filter to identify us. Look for the green light immediately ahead of you when you run off the bridge, which is where we will have cover and weapons for you. For now, let's try the over-the-hood exit."

It was a good thing that they practiced this because it took a few runs for the drivers to figure out how to get quickly onto the seat, and then over the dashboard in the correct position to slide to the front of the hood and drop to the road. Eventually they had it down.

A similar exercise was conducted with the palace breaching truck. This was done with the full team onboard because dismounting quickly was a critical element. The truck bed was set up with two benches, each facing the outside edges of the truck. The team could bail out directly over both sides, all at once. The practice involved reversing the truck to hit a row of barrels, then offloading the team members who immediately dove to the ground, well away from the sides of the truck. It was a bit easier than the bridge operation, and it only took four runs to master it. It took longer to rig the truck with the linear-shaped charges, however. Sabi had already had a frame welded to the back of the truck that was the width and height of the truck but came down to within less than twenty-five centimetres of the pavement.

Sabi rounded up the palace crew.

"We are going to take a test run to the area of the palace. I just want to make sure before putting in the detonators that we aren't going to have any issues getting the truck to the site with the weight of the team on board. Don't bring weapons; for this run you are just weights, so we can see how the truck behaves and make any changes to the route if there are problems."

The team mounted up and made a slow drive through town and behind the palace. There was one area where a large pothole caused the truck to settle low on one side and the newly-installed frame dragged on the road. Sabi was in the cab with the driver.

"You need to guide the truck around that hole when we do the real run. I don't want to risk any damage to the charges or the frame."

"No problem, Sabi, I didn't realize how deep it was, there is a way to get around it."

Of course, the day was also spent weaponing-up. The whole crew was familiar with the small arms, the heavier machine guns, and the RPGs. None of them had worked with noise suppressors before. Those that would be carrying weapons with suppressors practiced at a temporary indoor setup in the warehouse.

One of the mercs had driven front-end loaders and took time to get to know the loader that Sabi had obtained.

That evening, Sabi and Dan provided wine and beer for the whole crew and let them know that tomorrow was go day.

After the whole-crew session broke up, the three Canadians and Sabi continued to talk.

Sabi spoke first.

"So, Afghanistan, all three of you. That must have been hairy. Full-on combat mixed with IEDs and ambushes, I imagine."

"It was, Sabi," said Dan. The three of us were all there, but in different roles. Alida on artillery, Max was armour, and I was infantry."

"Armour? You had tanks in Afghanistan?"

"Yes, only the Canadians had tanks and they were lifesavers. In addition to firepower, they had a huge psychological impact on the Taliban. They were shit-scared of the tanks. One time, my unit got locked into an ambush in a hopeless valley, with steep rocky walls with the Taliban firing down on us. Some of the LAVs were hit and we had limited space to manoeuvre. Then Max's gang showed up with the Leopard 2s. They started direct fire into the hillsides and into a cluster of buildings that had a concentration of the Talib. Man, the hillsides started coming apart and the adobe-type buildings almost vanished. In minutes, enemy firing stopped and there was a mad scramble of retreating Talibs."

"How did you use artillery? My understanding is that there were a lot of hit-and-run attacks, making it hard to bring artillery to bear."

Alida responded.

"True, there weren't many set-piece battles. A few, where artillery really made a difference, but not that many. We did use artillery when we had good intelligence on Taliban gatherings or facilities. We had Excalibur shells, so with good intel, we could put the fire exactly where it was needed."

Sabi continued.

"I never heard much about Canadians in Afghanistan. I was told that it was all US and Brit."

"That's normal," said Dan, "we didn't have the size of the Americans, but we were there from day one, with special forces and as we brought in more units, we were assigned one of the hotspots – Kandahar Province. With its border with Pakistan, it was a very leaky area and hard to control. The Talibs just shifted back and forth across the border."

"Well, I'm glad that you guys have the experience," said Sabi. "I like your plan and am glad to have you here. Here's to tomorrow."

Everyone raised their glasses.

"Tomorrow!"

Chapter 18

1 July - 08:00 - 19:00

Early morning on coup day, we started things in motion. After a brief session with Sabi and the captains, Max kicked things off.

"Those assigned to the access denial crew with me, listen up, now. You will see a stack of yellow construction hard hats and yellow vests on my left. Let's get them on."

"Here's the plan. You are a road construction crew, improving the drainage on the road that runs from the Presidential Guard base into town. The backhoe will be cutting trenches across the road, one lane at a time, so that traffic can continue to flow. You will be laying concrete drainage pipes not far below the surface. These are, in fact, IEDs that we have prepared. As each pipe is laid, Sabi will be installing detonators and laying det cord connected to an ignition point. The det cord will simply be covered with dirt, and it will only be in place for a few hours. You will need to be careful when backfilling not to damage the detonators or cords, so you will backfill by hand, and finish off with cold mix asphalt."

"When this is complete, you will set up Claymore mines in the ditch on the north side of the road. Tonight, for the route denial we will be set up on the south side. The Guard are not combat troops that would attack into an ambush, and we therefore believe that they will try to escape away from us and take up firing positions in the north side ditch."

"As a last step, dump trucks will be laying down a berm of gravel about one hundred metres south of the road. These will be our firing positions tonight, which we will take up just prior to 19:00. Any questions?"

"Mike, for the denial, what is the plan, how will we be armed?"

"Given the size of the Guard, we expect that if they really get moving to get into the city, there will be four or five vehicles. You will be setting up five IEDs along the main access road. We will mark the location of each IED with a lantern because it will be dark when the Guard moves. As their expected convoy reaches the target area, the IEDs will be activated individually, and hopefully directly under each vehicle. We will have ten or more RPGs with us, as well as our AKs. Once the IEDs are blown, we will deal with any surviving vehicles or Guard members that way. The Claymores that you will lay will also be linked with det cord and have radio-controlled ignition. After a pause to allow any survivors to hit the ditch, these will also be set off. Immediately after that, we will assault the road and clear out any remaining Guard."

"I will not be with you this morning, because a white dude on a road crew in Doadja would stand out like a hooker at a wedding. I will be leading you tonight, because Sabi will be busy leading the palace assault team."

"Be careful out there this morning, don't work too hard or fast – we want it to look like a typical government crew."

That remark got a few chuckles.

"See you all this afternoon."

It turns out that a policeman did wander out from the nearby neighbourhood to chat, but really that was all it was – he was just putting in time. He wasn't particularly curious and after a brief back-and-forth and a smoke, he wandered back into town. Otherwise, it went exactly as planned.

By late afternoon, the road crew was back at the warehouse and everyone settled in for the routine of cleaning, checking, and loading weapons.

Sabi, the Canadians, and the captains gathered, and Sabi distributed satellite comm units. While the Canadians, except for Alida, camouflaged-up for the dark and to hide their whiteness, Dan briefed them all.

"We will be activating our own radio network at 18:30, because we are going to take down the national mobile phone network. I am assuming that GCHQ or the NSA may record all our network traffic, so we want to avoid leaving a trail that leads back to us, at least for the first couple of hours. Remember to use your designated callsigns. At each key point in your action, let the whole team know of your progress. If there is a problem, report it to me, at Delta. Our whole network will hear the reports."

"Everyone will be on radios, your team members will use call signs that you assign based on your designator – for example, my team will be Delta One, Delta Two, and so on."

"I will be coordinating operations and redirecting resources if there is a problem in a particular area. In the event of a serious failure, we will meet back here at the warehouse. From here, we will take a BMP that we have out back and make a run to the airport, or through the national park to the border."

At 15:00 Dan received a plain text message from Lare:

Out of Office – on holiday

This was the indication that he was enroute to Doadja on the business jet.

From 17:30 on, for about an hour, teams loaded up and moved out. Alida left first, because her initial task was to deal with the air force at the airport. When she was ready to assemble her team, she joined the other leaders in the command centre – just a table in the warehouse offices away from where all the troops were getting ready.

Dan immediately noticed how she was dressed.

"Whoa! You look like you are going to a banker's convention, not a gunfight, Alpha."

She was dressed in a sharp suit, carrying a Louis Vuitton satchel, and dripping with bling jewellery.

"Good, that was my intent. I want to look like a very prominent, extraordinarily rich African woman. After we cut through the fence, I am just going to walk right into the air force hangar, as if I just deplaned from a bizjet, looking very confused, and asking for the whereabouts of my limousine. My plan is to keep the guards focused on me while the team takes them out. Then, we will just zip tie all the others – pilots, ground crew, et al, and lock them up in one of the rooms there. We only need an hour of control."

"You will be pretty exposed during the walk-in."

"Sure, but they will be so worried that I am the wife of somebody important, that they will hesitate to do anything. Even speaking English will throw them off. They may think I am a Nigerian politician or something similar."

"Be careful, and of course, good luck."

Her team came up behind her. They were in combat gear with vests and had weapons with suppressors. Alida gave a wave and started to head out.

"Bye, guys, you be careful, too, see you on the other side."

18:00

By 18:00, it was already getting dark. Alida and her team had cut through the fence at a point between the FBO and the air force hangar and were in position to move. Her plan worked like a charm. As she neared the hangar from the apron side, the two sentries sitting on either side of the open hangar door noticed her at the last minute and in a jumble of grabbing rifles, they stood and shouted what would clearly be the Doadjan equivalent of halt. She loudly said in English, as she kept walking toward them:

"Where is my car? You need to help me. President Obissey said he would send a limousine to meet me, what the hell is wrong with this country?"

As she continued to walk, she placed a cell phone up to her ear. By this point she was walking between them into the hangar and they both turned to follow her. At that point, there were the muffled sounds of struggles behind her as her boys took out the two guards with trench knives. She paused briefly, to let them regroup, then walked into the ready room, where the pilots, ground crew were having dinner, served by kitchen staff behind an open counter. With her team right behind her as she came through the door, all she said was:

"All up!"

She then indicated with her hand that everyone was to stand up. One of the mercenaries quickly went into the kitchen area to make sure that there were no surprises behind the counter. He ushered the two staff he found, to go into the ready room. Everyone was frisked, and weapons, phones, or anything that could be used as a cutter, were confiscated. They were all then handcuffed with zip ties. Alida pointed to a storage room and the ten people were shuffled inside and their feet were also secured with zip ties.

Alida then directed one of the mercs who she knew spoke Doadjan.

"Tell them they will not be harmed and will only be restrained for an hour or so. If they make any attempt to escape, they will be shot."

Two of the mercenaries went back into the main part of the hangar. One took a bolt cutter from his backpack, the other a flashlight. Going into the open landing gear bays on the two old Mig21, the severed the hydraulic lines on the landing gear jacks.

With task one completed as planned, Alida radioed in:

"Alpha for Delta, hangar under control."

"Delta, Roger."

18:20

Alida left one of the mercs to guard the people in the hangar while she, Patrice, and the other two mercs went out the back of the hangar and followed the fence line to the base of the control tower. It was unguarded but had a metal door with a keypad for access. She quickly fired off a series of instructions:

"Just use the pry bar, this looks like it will pop easily. It may make a noise, so we need to hustle as soon as we pop the door. Patrice, if it makes a noise, you scramble as fast as you can up the stairs. If it is quiet, we will walk up at a normal pace, quietly. As soon as you reach the cab, have everyone stand and move away from the consoles. Ferdinand, you take up a controller position and assume controller duties. I don't expect any traffic except our own flight, but just allow whatever comes and goes to be treated normally."

As expected, with one boost under the lock area the door sprung open, with only a small metallic click.

"Okay, quiet approach," said Alida, and they all walked up to the tower cab.

The two crew in the tower had their backs to the stairwell and were chatting, so the tower takeover was quick and bloodless. The controllers made no attempt to reach for their radios when the armed mercenaries emerged and were completely compliant as they were restrained with zip ties and taken back behind the stairwell. Alida repeated the message she had given in the hangar.

"Guys, you will not be harmed, and we expect that you will be restrained here for only for an hour or two. Just relax, make no noise, and don't give us any reason to shoot you."

She radioed in again:

"Alpha for Delta, tower under control."

"Delta, Roger."

For Alida, it was now a waiting game with Lare scheduled to arrive in another ten minutes at 18:40. It wasn't long before an inbound business jet sought permission to land. It was Lare's flight. Alida left her tower team, walked back to where she had left the car, and drove to the FBO. Shortly after that, an older model Challenger 300 rolled up in front of the little building and an immigration officer wandered out to meet the aircraft. Potentially, this was a tense moment, because if Lare was on a Doadjan watch list, immigration might get involved. Alida was ready to act in that case. Her Vuitton bag contained a Russian MP443 with a suppressor.

No worries, after a brief look at his passport at the base of the jet's stairs, the agent handed Lare his passport back and he headed back into the terminal. Once the agent was inside, Alida called in a message to the whole team.

"Alpha for Delta, Newby is here."

"Delta, Roger."

"Mr. Lare, I am Alida, Nadeem's daughter. Please come with me. We are going to the government communications centre."

Lare looked nervous. He was pale and sweating.

"Mr. Lare, this is all going to be fine, the first steps are already seamlessly completed. You have an effective team acting for you. Just be ready for your interviews and to become President Lare."

Lare smiled nervously but said nothing. They got into the car and headed for town.

Now, it was all unfolding quickly. All the teams had dispersed, and within a brief quarter hour, it was all going to hit the fan.

· · · · · · · · · ·

18:50

Adan's four-person team took a car to a point close to the homes of the high-priced help – the heads of the Guard and the army, then using the darkness, walked into the target. The two houses were side-by-side, each with a sentry box in front. It was too easy, the sentries were seated, and as the mercenaries reached the perimeter of the lighted areas, they tried to stand up, but at that fifteen-metre distance, they were cut down silently by the suppressed weapons the mercs carried. The two mercs then headed into the first house. The front door wasn't even locked. They simply walked in, found the family gathered in the dining room, and cut down all of them in seconds.

The second house was even easier. Through one of the two large front windows in this big colonial era home, they could see the occupants gathered for dinner, with a cook coming and going from the kitchen. They simply waited for the cook to be in the dining room, then in a fusillade through the front window, took them all out. They turned and walked back to the car. The only noise had been from the collapsing window and these large homes were far apart in heavily treed yards. No one came out from any of the adjacent houses.

"Bravo for Delta, head honchos under control."

"Delta, Roger"

· · · · · · · · · ·

18:50

The government communications centre, with its centralized control of telephone, mobile phone, radio, TV, and Internet was the next target. These functions were centralized for ease of government control. It did create a unique vulnerability, however. The coup needed control of that operation before the planned 19:00 palace and bridge assault.

The centre is a large compound, right in the centre of the city, only about two klicks from the palace. It has a guarded gate on the perimeter fence, a separate smaller building containing the supplementary power units (SUPUs) to keep the systems on air in the event of a national electricity network failure, and a large hub building with servers and radio and TV production facilities. This windowless building has a single, steel door entryway.

Because of the set-up of the centre, it would not be enough to cut the external power; the SUPUs would need to be prevented from starting up as well. The other constraint is that the team needed to gain entry without any warning messages going out.

Four Presidential Guards were on duty at the gate to the compound. Leaving their truck, a block away, Dan and his four-member mercenary team approached on foot. One member of the team, Patrice, had experience with high voltage power and knew how to shut down the power and the SUPUs.

It was a walk-through type of guard house, with access to the compound through the building. People entering the compound would show ID, leave their ID and mobiles, etc. A large window allowed the guards to see who was approaching. All four guards were in the guard house.

In a whisper, Dan briefed the team on the final movements.

"There are four guards on duty. We will approach until we are near the perimeter of the lighting and shoot from there. Everyone, check that suppressors are on. Watch for my signal to stop moving forward and to shoot. Delta One, take on the first guard on the left, Two, take out the next one, Three, the next one, and Four, take out the guard on the right. We need to be sure they are down quickly so no alarms go off. Let's move!"

They approached in a fanned-out formation. Dan raised his hand to stop the team, then raised his weapon.

"Now."

The four shots were so close together that it was hard to even tell that there were four. The only loud sound was from the window hits, but there were only holes; the glass didn't shatter and fall. At a run, Dan led the group through the door and quickly checked all four guards to ensure that they were really gone.

"Four, to the power unit, others with me."

Delta Four raced across the compound to the power building, pulled bolt cutters from this pack, and cut the lock off.

"Delta for Delta Four, tell me when you are ready to cut power, then wait for my go."

Dan and the remaining mercs took positions at the main building door.

"Guys, night vision on."

Two or three minutes passed.

"Delta Four for Delta, ready here."

"Delta, go Delta Four."

Suddenly the fence and door flood lights went out. The four at the door waited with weapons raised. As expected, after a minute or two, the door opened and a man stepped out holding a flashlight. One of the mercs took him to the ground, while Dan and the other two raced in and found their way to the studio and the servers. The hallways were dimly lit by feeble battery-operated emergency lighting.

"Delta Three for Delta."

"Delta."

"Server area clear, there was no one here."

"Roger."

In the studio they found TV on-screen presenters and the technical crew, all frozen in the darkness.

"Two, tell them in Doadjan that we will not harm them if they do as they're told. No one is to touch any panels or mics unless directed."

Dan waited while Delta Two gave them instructions.

Dan now spoke the lie that he expected would be true in the next half hour.

"Tell them that there has been a change of government, that Obissey and the commanders of the Presidential Guard and army are all dead and that shortly they will be releasing a taped message to the nation."

He waited again as Two told them. Not surprisingly, there were a couple of smiles and exchanged glances. Not everyone thought that this was bad news.

"Also tell them that the new president will be here shortly and will be doing a live interview with you on TV and broadcast on the radio. You will know him and you can ask him anything you like about the future of Doadja."

Now, the only thing to do was to wait for 19:00 and for Lare's arrival at the studio with Alida.

"Delta for Alpha, Bravo, Juliet, Oscar, Mike, Sierra – the TV is off."

All the team leaders quickly acknowledged.

The teams had headed out by 18:45 and were positioning for 19:00. The original plan drafted by Dan was being followed. At seven p.m. all the teams would spring into action.

Just before seven p.m., Alida brought Lare into the broadcasting studio. The reactions of the staff there were interesting for the Canadian team to watch. Several of the TV journalists knew exactly who Lare was and greeted him with smiles and handshakes.

Dan spoke to the group:

"Soon after seven p.m., I will tell you to broadcast this taped message on Radio and TV. Although Mr. Lare is here and could speak live, if we use the tape, it will give President Lare and the on-air team time to prepare for a live Q&A session. You will have fifteen to twenty minutes to prepare."

Chapter 19.

I July 19:00

Two full dump trucks were making their way along the waterfront, heading for the bridge to Wailing Island. At seven p.m., the two trucks drove past the bridge road, stopped, and then reversed onto the bridge; first one, then the second. It was a tight enough fit that it required skill in getting them side-by-side on the bridge. Their practice had paid off. As the second truck came to a stop, a sentry started to walk out from the gate to the garrison.

"Hey, you fools, what are you doing here? You are not allowed here, move those damn trucks out of here now."

Before he could reach the trucks, both drivers fired the charges that blew the back wheels off the trucks and they collapsed onto the bridge. The two mercenary drivers bailed out over the hoods and ran for cover where Olivier and three other mercenaries handed them their weapons.

"Oscar for Delta, the bridge is closed."

"Delta, Roger."

A strange calm settled over the area, as the army sentries tried to figure out what was happening. In that calm, first the sound of small arms fire then the sound of a loud explosion shook the city. Clearly the palace breach was underway.

· · · · · · · · · ·

The palace team had left the compound with the others and slowly made its way to arrive at the back of the palace at exactly 19:00. There were two vehicles, an SUV to drop off the frontal courtyard attack team, and the weaponized stake truck to breach the rear wall of the palace.

At the palace, the diversionary assault on the front gate kicked the attack off. Although the frontal team was only seven

183

people, they were executing a plan to make it seem much larger. They poured AK fire into the gate house, supplemented by the deeper sounding fire of a 50 cal and a couple of RPGs.

As soon as the main assault team heard the automatic fire from the front of the palace, they backed the truck up as planned, off-loaded the troops, and fired the charges. The noise was deafening. Much of the concrete wall disintegrated into a cloud of dust and larger pieces were blown inward, into the palace.

"Up, go, go, go," Sabi led the team into the palace. The breach worked well, the wall was gone almost to ground level, with a few pieces to dodge around on the run in. Because it had been rehearsed, the team split up inside the hallway exactly as planned, with two of the mercenaries heading right to secure the private "safe room" area of the President, and the others all heading left down the hallway. Thankfully, the hand-drawn sketch was reasonably accurate.

According to that sketch, the first and only door on that first stretch of hall opened into the dining room. While most of the mercs went straight past that door and headed toward the front of the palace, Sabi and Sierra Two charged through the door. They came face-to-face with Obissey and his wife who were already up and running toward the secure private area.

Only a second passed before Sabi and the merc fired. At that range there was no chance of missing. and the two Obisseys were shot, and they both dropped to the floor. Sabi stepped forward and shot each of them in the head.

"Sierra for Delta, the leader is down, we are moving on securing the building."

"Delta, Roger."

At the centre of the room, holding a tray, a serving woman had frozen on the spot. Sabi and merc ran past her and headed to the other main dining room doors that led into the larger public spaces of the palace.

As the main palace assault team members worked their way toward the front of the palace, they ran into little opposition. The attack and noise from the frontal diversion had drawn all except two of the guards toward the front. The main team from the breach easily dealt with these two. There were various civilian staff, but they raised their hands or simply stood in shock. When Sabi met up with the frontal team he took a quick inventory.

"Two, any casualties?"

"One of our guys is dead, Sabi, and two are wounded."

"Bring the wounded into the palace and look after them. We have one wounded as well."

"Sierra for Delta, the building is secure. We have four casualties – one dead, three wounded."

"Delta, Roger."

As soon as Dan heard that, it was time to power up the comm centre and get the message out.

"Delta for Delta Four, power on now."

"Delta Four, Roger."

The lights came on in the comm centre and Dan handed over the video message on a thumbdrive and barked out some instructions. "Play this now, as fast as you can get your systems up. Please also put it out on the government website right away."

"People of Doadja, this evening the Government of Doadja has been removed. A new, temporary government led by me, Rafael Lare, has assumed power and will serve Doadja until stability allows an election.

Please remain in your homes and await further details. I will be available shortly for interviews on television and radio. Members of the Presidential Guard, please surrender your weapons immediately."

• • • • • • • • •

Back at the bridge, it had become obvious to everyone from the gunfire and explosions that the city was under attack and the army had started to move in response. It took a while because they couldn't reach the General, since he was no longer among the living. However, about fifteen minutes after the merc team had blocked the bridge, a BMP came out of the gates, accompanied by twenty or so infantry on foot.

Olivier had been instructed to deny any movement off the island, so his team opened fire on that group before they reached the trucks. Two RPGs brought the BMP to a smoking halt, and the infantry started to scramble backwards through the gate while returning fire. The bridge team was well concealed among the piers, waste, and buildings. The return fire was initially ineffective.

Before long, however, the mercenary team started to take machine gun fire from a heavier weapon and one member was hit.

"Anyone see where that heavy machine gun is, we need to deal with it now," yelled Olivier.

"Olivier, top left corner of the fort at the top of the wall."

That was why it was effective; it was looking down on them from four or five storeys up. Olivier grabbed a sniper rifle he had brought with them and scanned the parapet of the fort. There it was, a small target, just the muzzle flash. Estimating where the gunner must be crouched above the flashes, he slowed his breath and then fired. The firing stopped – direct hit. But there must have been at least a couple of soldiers up there, because almost immediately, the machine gun was back in action and the area around the mercenaries was being chopped up with bullets. Pieces of brick and wood were breaking off all around them. Dan set up and fired again. This time, the machine gun fire ceased for good.

There was intermittent AK fire coming from near the gate for a few minutes. That was cover for another breakout attempt, as a platoon size unit of soldiers rushed out of the gate and attempted to get between, and alongside, the damaged dump trucks. Backlit by the gate floodlights and forced into single file formation as they tried to pass between the blocking trucks, the soldiers were rapidly turned back by the mercenary fire.

After a couple of minutes, fire from the casern completely stopped and an officer came out of the gate waving a white flag and holding a megaphone. As he approached, Olivier could see he was a Major. Warily, Olivier stood and walked to the city-end of the bridge and the Major slid through, in between the two trucks, and addressed Olivier.

"We have just heard on the radio from Two Brigade that President Obissey is dead and that Lare has seized the government. Is that true?"

"Yes, sir, we have seized the airport, the air force, the palace, the communications centre, and are currently dealing with the Presidential Guard."

"What does 'dealing' with the Guard mean?"

"We have an effective ambush underway and expect there to be few survivors."

"We cannot raise General Yalumba, is there a reason?"

"He is no longer with us, either. Who is next in the chain of command?" Olivier asked.

"Colonel Oluda who is here in the garrison."

"What is his intent now?"

"Honestly, it is so confusing that I cannot answer that. He is in radio contact with Two and Three Brigade and they are developing their plan. Is there anything I can tell him?"

Olivier continued, "Advise him to watch TV or listen to the radio, and not to take any instant action to mobilize the three brigades. Our understanding is that the army has been subordinated to the Presidential Guard in the past and was not fully supportive of Obissey. The Presidential Guard will cease to exist as of today. If you have reason to believe that Lare will lead a reasonable government or even be an improvement on Obissey, we are asking the army to stand down. In fact, we could use your help to maintain public order and to round up and detain any surviving Guard members.”

“I will pass your message to the colonel.”

“Thank you, major,” Olivier said as he turned and walked back to his protected position.

The major went back into the fortress. No fire resumed from the island.

After waiting a few minutes, Olivier reported in.

“Oscar for Delta, the bridge is quiet. They are paying attention to Newby announcements. We have one dead. More information will follow.”

“Delta, Roger.”

• • • • • • • • • •

At the communications centre, Lare had been set up in the TV studio and was ready to go live. The interviewer was Andrea Adade, the most prominent TV personality in Doadja and a face well known to the public. When Andrea indicated she was ready, the taped message stopped, and they went directly to live programming.

“Good evening, I have with me President Rafael Lare. Mr. Lare, can you tell us what has happened?”

“Of course, Andrea. Earlier this evening, the Palace was seized and Obissey was removed from power, along with the top leadership in the army and the Presidential Guard. The army has already recognized the new government, but a few Guard soldiers are still fighting the new government team on the edge of the city.”

Lare then moved his gaze from the interviewer and looked straight into the camera:

“I now have a message for all citizens, but particularly those Guard members. I know that there is bitterness about the murders and tortures performed by the Guard on behalf of the ex-president, but revenge is not our intent. We will establish a Truth and Reconciliation Commission to record those crimes and to provide justice, but we will not be revengeful. Members of the Presidential Guard, I implore you to lay down your arms now, or risk an unnecessary death."

"Mr. Lare, you mention your team, who is on your team?"

"Andrea, you can appreciate that the actions of today required the utmost secrecy. A small group of fighters from Doadja and a few other countries undertook this operation. The team isn't as important as the outcome. In the next day or two, I will be announcing my cabinet and key government officials."

"Were any foreign countries involved – France, Spain, the US?"

"No foreign governments participated in this change of government, Andrea."

"Mr. Lare, can you describe your government?"

"Andrea, as an overview, I can tell you that it will be unlike anything the people of our country have seen for the past forty years. Our country is wealthy, but the people are poor. The new government will publish information on our oil revenues and we will be using those revenues to provide reasonable levels of health and education to the people. My biggest concern is that expectations may become too high. There is indeed wealth, but it takes time to build the hospitals and schools and other infrastructure that we promise. It will take time to train the doctors, nurses, and teachers and make their impact felt."

"Building an economy that serves our people will take years, but we need to start with health and education."

"My intent is to have a government that represents all Doadjans, not a single tribe or family. I also intend to have a government in which any type of corruption is a crime. I know it will take time to root out the culture of corruption that has eaten away at our country, but I will start at the top."

Once again, Lare looked straight into the camera:

"People of Doadja, I ask you to please be calm through the disruption of the next few days as we put our new government in place. It will be a government to serve you, the citizens of Doadja, not itself."

"Thank you, President Lare, I look forward to further opportunities to discuss your plans in the coming days."

"Thank you, Andrea."

· · · · · · · · · ·

Out on the highway that leads from the Guard base, the members of the fake road crew had started to pack up and move into their ambush positions. They had pretended to do road work until around 18:30, and then slowly started to disperse. A truck with their weapons and gear made its way in the gathering darkness and stopped in the field beyond the berm that they had constructed earlier. Two of the dump trucks made their way into positions to block off the highway at the right time to prevent civilian traffic from accidentally getting into the ambush. The road crews left lamps on the work site and slowly walked across the field to meet the truck. Just prior to 19:00, in the darkness, they removed their reflective vests, put on their combat gear, and checked their weapons.

As expected, whether it was the explosions and gunfire in the city, or a radio connection with the army that had triggered it, a small convoy emerged from the Guard base – a BMP followed by three trucks. As soon as Max saw them, he called it in. Exactly as planned, one of the dump trucks blocked the outbound lane to keep civilian traffic from leaving town and getting into the target area.

"Mike for Delta, we have traffic from the countryside."

"Delta, Roger, manage that traffic, Mike."

The Presidential Guard convoy had cut off inbound civilian traffic when it turned into the highway. The convoy was moving more slowly than the other traffic, so a gap opened in front of it as the civilian traffic pulled away. As soon as the last of this civilian traffic had passed by the dump truck barricade, the driver pulled it all the way across the road and then bailed out, racing to the berm to join the other mercenaries.

The critical hit was the BMP because it had a manned heavy machine gun. It would be extremely dangerous if it wasn't taken out. The IED closest to the city would be used to hit the BMP. If it missed, there wouldn't be a second chance.

Max and the mercenary crew waited tensely as the vehicles approached the IED locations. They had left a traffic cone and lantern by each one, marking the spot.

The gunner on the BMP did not seem to be aware of a potential threat enroute into town, he was looking straight ahead down the road. As this armoured personnel carrier was passing the marked area, Max triggered the IED:

"Hit," yelled Max as the vehicle jumped in the air with a flash. The group opened fire.

The remaining IEDs had been placed guessing at the distances between the convoy vehicles. That worked well for the first truck, as it stopped right on top of the next IED and went up in a ball of flame. It didn't work as well, for the other two, which stopped a distance from the IED marks. The mercs triggered them in any case, to add to the chaos, but the whole team was pulverizing the trucks with machine gun fire. The team fired three RPGs at the remaining trucks, with hits on the second and third units. They could see a scramble of Guard members bailing out of the last truck and, as anticipated, running away from the ambush into the ditch on the north side.

Max waited, giving time for the guards to hit the ditch, and then he triggered the Claymores. As soon as those exploded, he stood up and gestured with his arm.

"All, come with me, let's rip into them. Let's go"

The mercenary team jumped to their feet, and walked quickly forward toward the convoy, firing as they moved. There was sporadic fire from the convoy, and three of the mercenaries dropped, either wounded or dead.

When they reached the convoy, they found a few Guard members that were still firing, and put them down, while the others surrendered. Within a couple of minutes, all firing had ceased and thirty Guard prisoners were seated on the road, disarmed.

"Mike for Delta, countryside controlled. We have one dead, two wounded."

"Delta, Roger."

"Delta for Oscar. Inform the leader at the bridge that the group from the countryside is of no concern. Ask for his help in managing the town."

"Oscar, Roger."

· · · · · · · · · ·

Olivier raised a white flag and once again walked to the city-end of the bridge to the island. A figure emerged from the island base gate, but it wasn't the major. As the walking figure drew closer, Olivier could see it was a colonel. As he approached, Olivier saluted.

"I am Colonel Oluda. What is the situation?

"Colonel, I have been directed to inform you that the Presidential Guard has ceased to exist as a force and that it is fully under our control. I assume that you have seen President Lare's speech and interviews. We anticipate that because the gunfire has stopped, within minutes from now the city will erupt in celebration and possibly some looting and revenge. Are you prepared to support the new government and move into the city and maintain the peace over the next day or two?"

"Yes, we are ready to cooperate. We all hope for a better future."

"Okay, please assume that you are the commanding officer of the National Military Force, effective immediately. Tell your troops and tell Two and Three Brigade officers that President Lare expects controlled behaviour from the army. People in the streets may be wild and celebrating, but make sure you manage it sensibly, without undue force. We need to start off by building trust with the people of Doadja."

"Understood."

"Okay, I have a couple of bulldozers that we can use to pull these trucks off the bridge. Give us fifteen minutes, then be ready to move. Please take this radio set that is on our frequency to maintain communication. I am callsign Oscar; you will be Foxtrot."

"Thank you, Oscar."

Olivier saluted. The Colonel returned the salute and walked back toward the gatehouse.

"Oscar for Delta. The army is onside and will be coming to assist as soon as I can clear the hiking trail. They have a radio and can be reached as Foxtrot. All leaders, be aware that the army callsign on our net is Foxtrot."

"Delta, excellent work Oscar. I will inform Newby that all plans are delivered."

· · · · · · · · · ·

Dan joined Lare in the studio, where he was off-air and chatting with the TV journalists.

"President Lare, all our plans are fully implemented. There is the start of celebrations in the streets. The army is supportive and will shortly be moving into the city to limit looting and any violence that may occur. You can speak directly to the new army leader on this radio, just refer to him as Foxtrot for now. By tomorrow morning we can end all this cover once you officially appoint him as army leader. As the army enters the city, they will coordinate with our teams. You may want to speak to the army leader yourself."

Lare nodded, so Dan took the handset;

"Delta for Foxtrot, we have the President to speak to you."

He handed the satcom handset to Lare.

"This is Foxtrot."

"Foxtrot, this is President Lare. Thank you for your support and understanding. I apologize for any losses that your unit suffered in this change. We planned this to minimize casualties, but it is likely that there were some."

"A few, President."

"Please inform their families that we will be providing for them. Also, please ensure that your troops understand that this is not simply a change of leadership, it is a change of approach. I will be working to bring all our groups together to use Doadja's mineral and oil wealth to benefit us all.

"Understood, Mr. President. Your family's reputation speaks to that."

"Thank you. I will be officially appointing you as head of the military tomorrow. I will inform you in the morning of the location where that will take place. Please ensure that in the next few days, the army acts with restraint and allows celebrations to take place if they are not violent."

"Of course, President."

"Until tomorrow."

Dan took the handset from Lare and continued the transmission.

"Delta for Foxtrot."

"Foxtrot."

"Foxtrot, our units are at the palace, both at the front and at the back, where we breached the wall. We also have units at the access road to town, at the airport tower and air force hangar, and at the government comm centre. We have informed them that you will be coming through the city to take over. Tell your troops to expect to see them. They are in full combat gear, including vests and helmets and wearing bright blue armbands. We need to avoid any friendly fire incidents during this transition. As your troops move in, ours will meet them, then withdraw, except for those at the palace. We will be protecting President Lare for the next day or two until we are certain that the situation is under control."

"Roger, Foxtrot."

As soon as they finished the radio calls, one of the radio journalists came into the room, smiling.

"We are getting reports from outside the city that parties have broken out everywhere. People were ready for a change."

Dan spoke to Lare.

"President Lare, Alpha and I are going to take you to the palace by truck. We would like to settle you in the secure area of the palace for tonight where we can protect you. Hopefully with daylight, things will be more stable."

Dan, Alida, and the mercenaries hopped into a civilian delivery truck. With Delta One driving and Delta Two in the passenger seat, and their helmets off, the truck looked like it was simply making a late delivery. Dan and Alida were in the back with Lare.

"Delta one for Delta, this is going to be slow, the streets are full of people. No problems, except that we need to move slowly in the crowd."

"Delta, Roger."

It took an hour to get to the palace. They pulled up to the breached wall because it was closest to the secure area of the palace. Four mercenaries were already guarding the area. Delta One had already told them to expect them, to avoid any friendly fire, so they were able to bring the truck up close to the breach.

Dan issued some instructions for the President.

"When we disembark, we are going to take you to the secure presidential area of the palace. Please lock yourself in until the morning. You have a radio connected to our network and there is a radio in the secure area connected to the army."

They climbed down from the back of the truck and Lare showed his open and friendly nature by greeting each one the mercenaries at the palace and thanking them for risking their lives to help his country.

In the corridor, before entering the door to the secure area, Dan stopped Lare.

"President Lare, this may be the last you see of your friends from a far away country. It is time for obvious foreigners to disappear. We will be leaving Doadja in the next day or two as soon as it is clear that all is okay. Until then, we will be keeping an extremely low profile. Sabi will be leading the mercenary team from this point on, and the mercenaries will leave Doadja this week as well."

"Dan, Alida, I don't know how Doadja can thank you all."

Dan smiled.

"Well, you need to pay the mercenaries or their families the promised success fees as a start."

"Of course, but what about you, your colleagues, your parents?"

"All we ask is that you get James Mackenzie out of the Wailing Island prison as soon as possible so that we can take him home. Other than that, simply honour your vision and turn this country into something better."

"Thank you both again. I hope to see you in the future. Please come as my guests."

Dan and Alida turned and walked back to the truck. Leaving the two members of the Delta team at the palace to support the other mercenaries there, they drove back to the JaMAC compound.

"How about a cold beer, Alida?"

"Great, I think we deserve it – justice triumphs again!"

Dan laughed, grabbed two beers from the fridge, and settled into a chair.

"Living the dream!"

Chapter 20.
Sabi – 2 - 3 July

The night of the coup was chaotic. After years of being under the Obissey family thumb, the people of Doadja cut loose. While most of this was about partying and celebrating the change, there were elements of revenge and some purely criminal activity.

We used two bulldozers to drag the blocking trucks from the bridge to the army base and prison. By the morning of the next day, the army was fanning out across the city and elsewhere in the smaller towns and trying to re-establish order. In Nambi, the handover from the mercenaries to the army was a mixed bag. The change at the communications centre, the airport, and the palace went well, but there was some confusion. At the highway scene of the firefight with the Guard, the army showed up in a BMP and fired off shots at the mercenaries who were guarding the site. Max prevented the troops from returning fire and after a few minutes of tension, things calmed down and the mercs left the site.

The public looted the Presidential Guard base and gutted the barracks and houses. The families of the Guards all vanished. Some may have returned to their villages, but likely some were murdered. There were families on Doadja who had reason to seek revenge on Guard members.

There was some looting in Nambi, mostly consumer items – TVs, radios, even refrigerators.

The army rounded-up Obissey *fonctionnaires* and held them at the partially ruined Guard base until President Lare instructed the army to release them. Some had been simply bureaucrats doing a job for the government of the day. Others had used their positions for personal enrichment and to bring grief to anyone who opposed them. In Lare's mind, a truth and reconciliation commission would be the place to deal with these people.

By late morning, Lare was firmly in control at the palace. He had the army bring Obissey's Chief of Staff, Austin, to the palace. Austin arrived looking scared.

"Austin, I am Rafael Lare, the new President. Thankfully, you weren't found by an angry mob and murdered during the night. You were the key enabler of Obissey and are very strongly associated with his autocratic and violent actions, so you are probably concerned about what happens to you next.

"We are going to have a new government, but a very inexperienced government. We could use your help in a transition. My proposal to you is simple: protection and amnesty for you in return for your full support and cooperation. Specifically, we are going to need to know about the government's finances and on which government staff members we can rely to competently assist us. Your choice is to accept this offer, or we will leave you to subsequently face a Truth and Reconciliation Commission for your acts as Obissey's Chief of Staff."

Austin looked visibly relieved. He knew he had just dodged a bullet.

"President, I never viewed myself as an enabler, just a humble public servant."

"Well, you need to do some soul-searching, Austin. What is your decision regarding support?"

"I will support your government and do whatever I can to enable an effective transition."

"Excellent. The first things I need are copies of all our agreements with oil companies, mining companies, and foreign fishing fleets, along with a picture of the revenues from these and where the revenues have been going in the past. I also want to know everything you know about how corruption may have tainted these revenues."

"Also, provide me as soon as possible with a picture of the government's overall revenues and expenses."

"Thirdly, we need immediate public servant support. Identify those who you know to be competent and useful and provide that list to me, along with any notes you can include on their skills and particular areas of knowledge."

"You will be working in the palace. I am meeting shortly with the people that will form our new government. I will inform them of my agreement with you regarding protection and cooperation. Of course, we will have more questions in the coming days. Please be aware that if I find that you are less than fully cooperative, I will not hesitate to terminate the agreement. That is all. Thank you."

"President Lare, I am very grateful for your forgiveness and generosity in allowing me to serve your government. I will do my best to serve you."

Later that day, Lare assembled the key players, including the interim commander of the army and a group of younger Doadjans that he had selected as an initial Cabinet. This group cut across all the tribes in Doadja. It was going to be a new image. Lare addressed the group.

"I have brought you all together because I want you to be part of my government. Immediately, I would like you to please help me in communicating that this is going to be a radical shift for Doadja. We are going to have an honest government focused on improving the basics for Doadjans. We are not a poor country, merely a country that has been impoverished by its leaders for decades. With the right knowledge, and the funds that we will have available, we can do better."

"I have asked Austin Mbaye to stay on to assist our government. I know that some of you may question this, given his close relationship with Obissey, but we need his knowledge of the public service and of existing relationships and contracts with the major oil and mining companies and with foreign governments. He has just given me his personal assurance that his one mission will be to serve the new government."

"There is one thing I want to make perfectly clear. Corruption at any level will not be tolerated and will be dealt with harshly. I will be setting up an anti-corruption bureau as part of a reconstituted police force."

"It is important that we don't raise expectations too high. When you talk to people, be sure to communicate that, first and foremost, we will be working to improve health and education, but that it will take time. They will need to be patient."

"In terms of responsibilities and immediate action, here is my initial plan. In ten days, I want each of you to give me your first ideas that we can go public with as to what our future direction will be in your area of expertise. It will be far from perfect, and it will incorporate assumptions to make up for missing information, but it will lay out the big picture as to where we want to go. Here are my initial priorities for each one of you:

- Robert, please take on Health. Quickly do the best you can to create an inventory of what we have in terms of facilities, doctors, nurses. Prepare a picture of where we want to be in five years, using good models from other developing countries - Botswana, or Vietnam, for example. Identify the gaps and prepare a road map of how we can get to our goals, along with a preliminary year-by-year budget.

- Education will be the responsibility of Francois. Like health, start with an inventory of where we are - literacy rate, completion of different education levels, availability of trained teachers. Then, identify where we want to be and how to get there, with budget estimates.

- Defence is Sabi. I want you to develop plans to eliminate the air force. It only existed to threaten our own people. Also, identify the resources we need to protect fisheries in our ocean economic zones. Prepare budget estimates for capital acquisitions and operations. Colonel Oluda, you are the Chief of the Defence Staff. Unlike in the past, you will report to a civilian, in this case, Sabi. The two of you will work together to develop a new vision for the military and related budgets.

- Fisheries will be Enrique Esroque. He is on his way in from the UK. I have directed Austin, the outgoing Chief of Staff, to provide us with all copies of our fisheries agreements. I suspect these may be ridiculous and we will have provided major fishing nations with access to our waters with almost no benefit to Doadja. State players will have provided benefits directly to Obissey in one form or another. Enrique will be directed to review these agreements, compare them to best practice agreements elsewhere and draw up a plan to renegotiate or terminate them, as necessary. He will provide an estimate of the impact of proposed changes on in-shore fishing, and on national revenues.

- Philip, I would like you to take on Industry. Please look at what we have and identify any areas where we may be able to create competitive advantage. Our labour costs are among the lowest in the world. Is there any way to gain advantage from that? What barriers are there to growth in terms of human resources, skills, etc? Identify opportunities with a plan and budget to get there. Also, oil and mines will be part of your area. Austin will be providing us with copies of all agreements with the oil companies and all mining agreements, which may suffer from similar issues as fisheries. Benchmark these against other countries and come back with recommendations on where we want to get to, how to get there. Provide a picture of current revenues and projected revenues with the proposed changes.

- Transport will be the responsibility of Omar Ngame, who will be joining us later this week. Omar is currently living in Paris. His portfolio will include ports, airports, and roads. I will brief him on his arrival, but he will be dealing with similar issues in that portfolio – inventory, objectives, gaps, strategy, revenues, expenditures, and budget."

"I know that you may be aghast at the scale of what I have asked you to do. This will only be our first cut and we will be working together to improve it over the next year or more, but it will give us a common picture of our potential revenues, and our potential costs. Then we can start to sort out priorities and gather more information."

"Austin has indicated that there are a dozen competent public servants that can assist us. I will be assigning these people to you later today. For now, we will all be working out of the palace. Because of the pace, and because we will be physically close together, I want to start each day with a very brief Cabinet meeting where we can quickly go through progress and challenges. Any questions?"

"President, what is our actual status?

"I want to hold an official Cabinet investiture in about two weeks. I would like to show the public who you are and what you are responsible for. By that time, we will all have drafted our initial action plans. In the meantime, I hereby appoint you as my interim Cabinet members. I will be sorting out pay and benefits in the next couple of days. I hope that none of you expect 'big man' pay and benefits. There will be no fleet of Mercedes in this government. We will all gear our remuneration to the performance of the country, increasing it as we go forward."

"I know that you will have questions, but we will have many opportunities over the next two weeks to talk individually and as a group. I may not be able to answer all your questions. You must know that, at this point, I don't know any more than you do. I am relying on your youth, and your commitment to Doadja to help us all get through this."

. . . .

Lare also called the warden of Wailing Island Prison while I was still in his office.

"Warden, this is President Lare. Do you know which of your prisoners are political and which are simply criminal?"

"Yes sir, we keep the politicals on a separate floor."

"Release the politicals today and call me back when you have done that. As for the criminal prisoners, I want a plan and budget from you by the end of the month to improve conditions for these people to a standard for diet and exercise that doesn't have them dying while in your hands."

"Yes, sir."

"Sabi, James will be released today. You may want to have someone at the prison to meet him."

"Yes, sir, and thank you for moving quickly on this."

"Sabi, don't forget my conditions on this. I want James gone from Doadja and all his companies here wound down as soon as possible. I do not want my name associated with his in the people's minds."

"Understood, sir."

I went to the prison myself and waited at the end of the bridge. Around two p.m., a group of thin, dishevelled, bearded men shuffled out of the garrison gate and slowly made their way across the bridge. Even in their filthy state, James was easy to pick out as the only white guy. He saw me and stumbled straight into my arms.

"God, Sabi, it is so good to see you! How did you manage to organize my release? I really thought that I was going to die in there."

"We killed Obissey and seized the country."

"Oh, jeez. Go big or go home!"

"Exactly, I will give you the full story later. You look like crap; you smell terrible and you are probably crawling with lice. I am putting you in the bed of the truck to take you to get cleaned up, fed, and rested. We can talk in a couple of days about what went on and what's going to happen now."

I took James to his house, where his housekeeper, cook, and a nurse were waiting to bring him back to the real world.

"Listen James, just rest, eat, and get cleaned up. I will be back tomorrow afternoon."

· · · · · · · · · ·

Late the next day, over tea, I filled James in.

"James, the story is stranger than you can imagine. After I found out where you were, I met with Austin, then Obissey, and it was clear that there was no intention of ever releasing you. I kept up the monthly cash flow to Obissey, prayed he wouldn't seize me and the JaMAC assets, and hid/dispersed our inventory as quietly as I could.

"I knew that a prison break was unrealistic, but then old friends of yours got involved and it escalated from there."

"What old friends?"

"Nadeem Nawaz, Matthew Hawney, and their children."

"Their kids?"

"Well, very much adult kids – all military or ex-military. The coup was the Canadians' idea. Dan Hawney, Matt's son, concluded that it was easier to take over the country than to pull off a prison break."

"Are they here?"

"Yes, but they're keeping a low, low profile. They were very much concerned that this should not look like a neo-colonial coup. For ops they were camoed-up and wore face coverings, but as soon as we got control, they vanished into the background."

"They have another Canadian special forces member with them. His name is Max Lapeyre. He was here to augment the team – came along out of loyalty to Alida and Dan, and because he loves a good shoot-up. Listen, I will take you to meet them the day after tomorrow, you need to take it easy until then. When we are all together you can get all the details."

"Sabi, you couldn't have pulled this off with just you and a handful of Canadians. What other resources did you have?"

"You know that we have the weapons and we have the network, so we assembled a force of about fifty mercenaries to help us out."

"Man, I am really going to have to get the details on this, it all sounds fantastic!"

"You take it easy right now, James. Just sleep and eat, and I will pick you up on Wednesday morning and take you to see your friends. We have turned the warehouse into a B and B."

"Will the mercenaries be there as well?"

"Maybe a few. We have started to exfiltrate them before the world press shows up here. See you Wednesday."

Chapter 21.
Alida – 4 July

We hung out in the warehouse for three days while James regained enough strength at home to travel. He was up and around on day two. On July fourth, Sabi brought him out to the warehouse after breakfast.

We were all having coffee around the table when they came in. James was wearing a big grin:

"Wow, it is great to see you, as you can imagine! Dan, Alida, how long has it been? I have seen your dads' a few times in the last couple of years, but you two have been all over the world. And you must be Max. Thank you all so much for risking your futures and your lives to get me out. I hope I will find some way to thank you more once we are out of Doadja."

"Sabi has given me some of the story, but I would love to hear more. Any coffee left?"

"Tell me what has happened, how I got released. I heard a firefight from the prison, including 50 cal and something like RPG or LAW fire. Did you break me out?"

I left it to Dan to explain, since it was his plan. Dan, Max, and Sabi were obviously happy to see James. I faked it, because I was glad that we had succeeded, but took little pleasure in seeing James.

Dan's story took an hour, and James' reactions were fun to watch – mostly disbelief and laughter.

"You overthrew Obissey, his Guard, and the Doadja military with a force made up of Sabi, three Canadians, and fifty mercenaries! Did I get that right?"

"That's it."

"And Obissey?"

"Obissey and wife did not survive the coup."

"Man, that goes beyond my wildest imagination, and I thought I was a boundary pusher! But, why the coup, and why you three?"

"Simple, the coup happened because we were convinced that a prison break wouldn't work and a coup might. Why? Because your old classmates Nadeem Nawaz and Matt Hawney didn't want to see you die in prison here. Why us? Because we had the skills to plan this and to pull it off with Sabi's help. Your old guy classmates were a little past their prime to pull it off themselves, so they brought Alida and I in."

James was stunned,

"Nadeem and Matt set all this up?"

"Well, the hard bits – the idea, and the recruiting of Lare," Dan said. "Sabi and the rest of us planned the details of the coup."

"Sabi wouldn't have dreamed of this on his own," exclaimed James. "Where did you three get the balls to be here for the action?"

Dan responded, "It's what we do, James. Max and I are active special forces today and Alida, although not military now, was with us in Afghanistan. We are all RMC grads."

"I knew that, Dan; at least about you and Alida. Both of you are following in the footsteps. Your dad and Alida's dad were great soldiers and great friends. Tell me about the mercs. Sabi, I assume you lined all that up?"

"Yes, James, you would know some of them, although there are a lot of younger ones mixed in; directly from the Congo in many cases."

"Were there casualties, Dan?"

"We were lucky that the Guard were so hopeless, but we still had three dead and five wounded."

"How did you pay them, Sabi?"

"You did, James, or technically it was JaMAC," said Sabi, as he started to laugh. Everyone else joined in.

"I did? There certainly wasn't enough in our local accounts to do that. With a team that size, we are talking, what, one or two million?"

It was my turn to speak:

"James, my specialty is financials. I accessed your offshore accounts and moved sufficient funds to pay the mercenaries into accounts here in Africa. My day job is a forensic accountant, often dealing with corporate fraud, including cases where people try to hide funds. I have the tools and skills to get into your accounts."

"Alida, it's embarrassing that you were able to do that, but sitting here today, it is hard to be critical. Would I have paid a couple of million to get out of that hellhole? For sure! It would have been easier if Obissey would take a bribe that size, but the trouble with billionaires is they get all snooty about a bribe of a million or two."

"Listen, everybody, I am still exhausted from my prison ordeal, and with everything that you have just told me, including about the looting of my bank accounts, I'm all tired out," James said, with a smile. "I am going to lie down for a while and get some rest."

Sabi then headed out to deal with the forced, rapid wind-down of the companies. I expect this would be informal, mostly just cleaning out accounts, trying to move the stock of weapons out of Doadja. The three of us just hung out at the warehouse, reading, chatting, and sleeping.

Later in the day, we heard noise from vehicles coming in on the gravel lot in front of the warehouse. The immediate thought was that there had been a counter coup and this was Guard or army coming for us. Everyone grabbed a weapon, including James, and we took cover behind crates.

A couple of minutes later, the warehouse door opened and a single army officer stepped in, unarmed with his hands clearly in view.

"My friends, President Lare is here and wishes to meet with you. Please put down all weapons and come forward."

There was no choice really, whether this was for real or a ruse, so we followed instructions. A half-dozen armed troops came in and looked around, checking out the warehouse. When they were done, Sabi and Lare walked in.

"Please, everyone, let's sit and talk," said Sabi. "Captain, you can move your troops outside and leave us. These are friends."

We waited until the soldiers were outside and the sallyport closed, then Lare began.

"Dan, Max, Alida, Sabi, I need to thank you all. Indeed, Doadja needs to thank you, but as discussed, we need to keep the involvement of foreigners as invisible as possible. I will be expecting you to leave Doadja as soon as possible. Tomorrow would be good."

"James, I am happy you are out of Wailing, but your business here is done. Doadja will no longer be poking its thumb in the eye of the world with its false end-user certificates and tolerating your operation in this country. I expect you to be on the plane with the other Canadians."

James nodded silently, accepting the inevitable; his eyes focused on the floor.

"Sabi, I am aware of the unsavoury history of the businesses that you and James had here but can overlook that, provided that your affairs here are immediately wrapped up. You cannot be the Minister of Defence and have these other dubious interests. I need someone on-point with the military who is not likely to try and seize the government in their own interests. I need you to commit to ensuring that the priority of the military is to serve the country."

"As discussed with Alida and Sabi, I have decided to pay the balance owing to the mercenaries or their families, but I want them out of the country as quickly as possible. Please thank them for their service. I know they did it for the money, but they still risked their lives, and the outcome will certainly be an improvement to our lives here."

"Please extend my thanks to Nadeem and Matt. I hope to demonstrate that their trust in me was well-placed. As you know, I have told the people of Doadja that improvements to their lives will not be overnight, but I hope to be able to create early signs of progress, particularly in children's health."

"Tell Nadeem and Matt that they will be receiving official invitations to the new government's investiture. I realize they may have to explain to someone how that came about, but I will leave that to their imaginations."

"Once again, thank you. Without you, this would not have been possible."

Lare stood-up, turned, walked to the door, and stepped outside without a backward glance. The five of us just sat there silently as the vehicles started up and left.

After a couple of minutes, James spoke:

"I suppose it is as good a time as any to retire. I need to stop by Canada and see Nadeem and Matt, but then I think I will just relax for a while in Mustique. You four will be welcome there any time. It is a little piece of paradise. You fly to Barbados, then take a little four-seater Aero Commander down to Mustique in an hour. I can't even get my jet in on the runway there, but the island is great. About forty homes, with a lovely beach on the east side. No crowds; you usually have the beach to yourself.

"Can someone lend me a working mobile? I need to call the pilot."

I told James that I needed to be dropped in Amsterdam on the way home.

"No problem, Alida, we need to fuel up in Europe anyway."

Sabi gave James his phone and James set up the flight out for the next day.

At the Nambi air terminal, there were soldiers hanging around, a few immigration officers, but no hassles, and we were airborne shortly after getting to the airport. The private jet was comfortable as expected, and we settled in for the seven-hour flight to Amsterdam.

When we rolled to a stop at the Aviapartner Executive FBO in Amsterdam, I got up and waited for the stairs to drop.

"This is me, guys. Thanks for the great adventure. I'll see you back in Ottawa."

"Bye, Alida, thanks for pitching in," said Dan to nods all around. James added, "Yes, thanks even for pillaging my bank accounts; it saved my ass!"

At the bottom of the stairs, there was a Dutch customs/immigration officer who checked my passport along with two other people dressed in suits. After checking my passport, they pointed me to the FBO, then all three boarded the plane, to check documents there.

I went into the FBO. Attractive white leather furniture, with big windows overlooking the apron. Instead of catching a cab or limo into the city, I decided to wait in the lounge. I could see the plane out the window, with the truck fuelling it for the leg across the Atlantic.

Within a couple of minutes, the Dutch officials came off the plane, with James locked in a set of handcuffs. They loaded him into a car that had pulled onto the apron. When the car left, I walked back out to the plane and got on board.

Dan and Max were surprised to see me back on the plane. Dan immediately asked,

"What's happening, did you see that they took James in handcuffs? Why are you back with us, I thought that you needed to be in Amsterdam for a meeting or something."

"Yes, I did see what happened to James, and I am responsible for that."

Well, that got their attention.

"You need to know what happened in Doadja when I was digging through James' stuff, looking to get into his bank accounts.

JaMAC was only one of James' interests. I soon discovered that he was also moving women and children from Africa into the sex trade in Europe. I couldn't handle that; I was not going to free a human trafficker. James has really hit bottom, guys. So, my options were to tell the whole team and shut down the entire coup-rescue, and suck it up and bring James home, or something in between. I gave the evidence that I found in James' accounts and on his computer to the Dutch police. They were the logical choice, since the other end of much of the traffic was through Amsterdam. Once they saw the evidence, I was able to cut a deal with them. They agreed to a maximum four years of prison for James in return for my help in shutting down the network and delivering the evidence and James to them.

"Holy crap, a human trafficker. Some friend your parents had," exclaimed Max.

"To be fair, they didn't know him as that. They knew he was an edgy guy, with the mercenary and arms trade stuff happening, but I am sure that this sex trafficking would come as a major surprise. In any case, guys, it is done. There is no value in even telling Matt and Nadeem. They will find out soon enough without us bringing it up. All we need to say is that Dutch officials took James off the plane."

"By the way, I made a couple of other substantial withdrawals from James' bank accounts. One transfer went to a charity in Holland that supports trafficked women, and the other one to a new charity set up in Canada to support and assist women to stay in school in Doadja."

I went to the cockpit and spoke to the pilot.

"James is delayed here. He said to take us home to Ottawa and he will call you later to bring him home."

"No problem, buckle up."

Postscript – Nadeem

In my role as Security Advisor to the Prime Minister, I was copied on anything that might relate to security that came into Global Affairs Canada. I obviously knew that James had been taken off the plane in Amsterdam, because the young gang told me as soon as they got back.

Two days after their return, a message came into GAC HQ from our embassy in The Hague:

A Canadian, James Mackenzie, was arrested on arrival by private jet at Amsterdam Schiphol Airport on 5 July, on charges of human trafficking. Mr. Mackenzie, who was based in Doadja until expelled as a result of the recent change in government there, allegedly was the African connection to European organized crime groups moving women, and girls as young as fourteen, from various African countries into sex work in Europe.

Police in Holland have made a point of crediting the assistance of a Canadian woman in providing evidence to support the case, which they had been pursuing for some time. Additional evidence may be provided by the new government in Doadja.

Hmm. Assistance from a Canadian woman. What was that about? I called Alida.

"Alida, I just got an email from Holland indicating that James has been charged with human trafficking and that a Canadian woman assisted in the case. Do you know anything about that?"

"Dad, I'm on another call right now, can we talk tonight? I will drop by your place. You may want to have Matt drop by as well."

"Okay, sweetie, see you this evening."

Alida came over around seven-thirty p.m. Matt was already there having a beer with me on the back deck.

"Hi, girl."

"Dad, Matt."

"Give us the story."

"Straight ahead. I am the woman referred to. I know James is your old friend, and I know the mission was to get him out of Doadja, but when I was going through all his files and electronic stuff, I discovered that in addition to the arms trade, he was leading a large-scale human smuggling operation, moving women and girls into Europe for organized crime there. The materials were clear and damning."

"For you, the judgement may be different, but for me the moral jump from his weapons trafficking to human trafficking was just too far. I could not be involved in freeing that wealthy criminal to live a luxe life while the women he trafficked continued to be abused."

"I met with Dutch national police on my way back from Doadja during that trip I did before the coup. It turned out that they were well aware of that trafficking, knew the European end, and had been trying to build a case for the past two years. The material I gave them filled in a lot of holes in their case."

"Because of your past friendship, I cut a deal with the Dutch that made James accountable but wasn't too harsh. In return for the evidence that they needed, they agreed not to pursue more than four years of jail time for James. In my mind, that struck a balance that worked for me. We still saved him from an early, horrible death. He can still go to his tax-free retirement in Mustique. But he had to pay something on his way there."

"Oh, that's not all. I also donated a million dollars out of his accounts to a support group in Holland that works with trafficked women and another million to a charity focused on the education of girls in Doadja. I suppose when he gets out of jail, he will notice that as well."

Matt and I sat silently for a while. It seemed like minutes, but who knows, it may not have been all that long.

"So, you decided not to share this with us, before you decided to share it with the Dutch police?" I asked.

Alida responded:

"Dad, Matt; I didn't want your advice on this. I knew that you would be conflicted and it would have really caused damage to our Doadja plan if you had advised me not to do it. I would have had to ignore you."

Matt jumped in.

"I think you might have misjudged us, Alida. We didn't know about any of that. To us, James was just an adventurer, living on the edge. We had no idea of how far down he had slipped. Had we known, we might have tried to think of different outcomes, including leaving him in prison in Doadja, but our judgement wouldn't have been so different from yours."

I added:

"Alida, I can't see how you could have acted differently. I always brought you up to be a moral person and I believe your time in the army would have enforced that. I fully support what you did, and I am so sorry that you were put in that position."

Alida let out a sigh.

"Well, that's a big relief, you two. I was praying that you would support me in the end, but I know how strong the bonds of personal loyalty can be. Well, now we can all watch it play out in Holland. Maybe the evidence will be insufficient. Maybe he will only get two or three years."

Over the following ten days, I watched for messages relating to Doadja security that were relevant to Canada. The only one that was a bit concerning was a note that Matt received at CSE from GCHQ raising a flag that there may have been Canadian involvement in the coup. Nothing of substance, just some key word bumps in emails and a few calls from Doadja that mentioned Canada, and a bit of sat phone traffic that seemed out of context. Nothing that worried me too much.

In mid-August, both Matt and I received official invitations to the investiture of the new Cabinet in Doadja. We both thought it wise to decline.

The Author

G. Burns Hamilton served as an army engineer captain in the Canadian Army and as an Assistant Professor at the Royal Military College of Canada. He has also been a lecturer at both McGill and Concordia universities. Burns has been Canada's representative on NATO's Civil Aviation Planning Committee and Planning Board for Ocean Shipping. The consulting company that he founded and led for twenty-five years, Sypher, has advised governments and private agencies in eighty countries, including many in Africa.

He is also the co-author of the first and second editions of *Global Megatrends and Aviation – the Path to Future-Wise Organizations.*

Burns lives in Ottawa, Ontario.